# HA
# AND I

# HAROLD
# AND I

*An Incredible Journey Consisting
of Supernatural Events*

## MARIE CHAPIAN

Text and Illustrations © Copyright 2007 – Marie Chapian

DESTINY IMAGE® PUBLISHERS, INC.
P.O. Box 310, Shippensburg, PA 17257-0310

"Speaking to the Purposes of God for this Generation and for the Generations to Come."

This book and all other Destiny Image, Revival Press, Mercy Place, Fresh Bread, Destiny Image Fiction, and Treasure House books are available at Christian bookstores and distributors worldwide.

For a U.S. bookstore nearest you, call 1-800-722-6774.

For more information on foreign distributors, call 717-532-3040.

Or reach us on the Internet: www.destinyimage.com

ISBN: 978-0-7684-2373-0

For Worldwide Distribution, Printed in the U.S.A.
1 2 3 4 5 6 7 8 9 10 11 / 09 08 07

# How It All Happened
# (Table of Contents)

# 1

## My Big Fat Move
## to Lake Clearbottom

My name is Bellflower Munch and I have a friend who happens to be an angel. The real kind. Like angel-from-God angel. Are you thinking I may be a little crazy in the head probably? Are you thinking angels don't come down from Heaven and visit 11-year-old girls? What I'm about to tell you happened to me, Bellflower Munch, and for positive certain I am telling you, angels are real. I better start from the beginning.

My totally pathetic beginning.

First off, I haven't always lived with my Great Aunt Twill in Lake Clearbottom, Minnesota. My real home was always with my mother in St. Paul. Maybe you've heard of these places. Well, maybe not Lake Clearbottom because it's a small town on an even smaller lake that most maps don't bother to point out. Great Aunt Twill says that's because it's a place known only to God and the weather. People in Lake Clearbottom always talk about the weather. In the summer it's beastly hot and in the winter it's ghastly cold. I should know. I arrived when the weather was getting cold, and believe me, I could have frozen my nose off.

But you probably want to know about the angel, so OK— but I warn you, be prepared. There was plenty of strange stuff going on in Lake Clearbottom. I bet if my mother knew what she was getting me into, she never would have left me behind and taken off for California to find her "authentic self" and create a so-called "decorous home" for us. (Decorous, she told me, means *proper*. She liked the sound of the word.)

Thunder Bay*
Hibbing*
Duluth*
St. Cloud*
Minneapolis*
St. Paul*
OH THERE
Lake Clearbott
Rochester*
see the (pinhead)
*nice places everyone knows

When I lived in St. Paul, my totally pathetic life consisted of watching TV, reading books, eating junk food, and wishing we had Internet like everyone else on the planet. My mother had just ended her wedding engagement to a certain Mr. Lars Lagleby, whom I never liked anyhow, and she decided she was going to broaden her horizons and head for Hollywood because a place like Hollywood was always in desperate need for talented hairdressers like herself. Besides, her girlfriend, Twila, from beauty school, was out there and said she'd help her "get a foot in," whatever that meant.

I didn't want to leave St. Paul. Things were going fine for me at school. I actually almost made friends, which wasn't easy considering how many times we moved and I'd be plopped down in another new school. The longest I was ever at one school was one semester minus three days; but in St. Paul I was on the verge of *belonging* somewhere because for some reason the most popular girl in the class liked me and invited me to a pajama party at her house. (I think it was because I happen to be extremely smart in English and I showed her how to tell an adverb from an adjective. Duh.) The pajama party was my big chance to be with kids my own age for an entire night. Besides that, I had racked up some big brownie points with my English teacher when I volunteered to erase all the pencil marks in the used textbooks the county sent us.

I told my mother with as much drama as I could muster that I didn't want her to take off for sunny old California, and weren't we *happy* in grayish old St. Paul?

That's when she decided to plunk me off at my Great Aunt Twill's and head for Hollywood without me.

"I'm sure you'll *like* your Great Aunt Twill," my mother trumpeted, as though pawning me off to live with an unknown relative was something to be excited about.

"How come I've never heard you mention Great Aunt Twill before?" I asked with my best pouty face.

"Certain family problems. But don't worry your little head; she'll take to you, Sweetie, I'm sure, I hope…that is, if you give her enough time. Besides…"

"Besides what?"

"I have no choice. No one else will have you."

What she meant was, we had no other family around and nobody she knew would know what to do with a smart 11-year-old kid like me under their noses for longer than a day or two.

"Flower, honey," (which is what she always called me—Flower). "Flower, honey," she said, "I want you to understand and appreciate my situation." She was using her "serious" voice. She bent down and put her face directly in front of mine to emphasize *how* serious.

"I have put a lot of *heart* and *effort* into finding the best place for you to stay while I'm gone. I know this is the *very best* choice I could make for you, for us. *Trust me*. It will just be for the *teensiest* little while, and then I'll be back for you. I promise! Try to understand!"

I gave her one of my deadly-poor-me stares which I practiced a lot in the mirror.

"You don't want me to ignore the open door of opportunity, do you?" she went on, getting emotional. "Don't you think your mother deserves a little recognition and happiness in this life?"

I stared at her, my face deadpan.

"Now honey, don't give me that look. Stop that! I hate it when you give me that look."

She was referring to my pathetic-poor-me stare.

*"Stop that right now!"*

I asked her, "How long will this success and recognition take?" I was wondering what I was supposed to do without a parental figure to show up at PTA meetings. Who'd sign my report card?

"Come off it, Flower!" my mother said, flipping a long strand of hair over one shoulder. "I *can't* take you with me. Please *understand* and be a *good* kid. I have to get *set up* and all. You know, get my *dream job*, find a place to *live*, get settled, find my *authentic self*. Then I'll be back for you. I promise."

"You just want to get rid of me," I said with one eye closed and peering at her between two fingers.

Then she said she had had it with me and my selfish, stubborn self. She had gone to great *extremes* making the best arrangements for me—that is, to stay with her Great Aunt Twill—and I wasn't even the least bit grateful. Here she was, a widow with a child to raise *alone*, and did I even *care* about her hardships?

She said there were things I not would understand until I was older, but she *had* to go on with her
life and find her authentic self—which she believed to
be in California. I was just a kid and what did I know
about life? This was her chance at success, and she
was not going to let it slip out of her hands like so
much sand—and, boom, off she went.

That's how I made the unfortunate move from
our apartment in St. Paul to Lake Clearbottom, and to
the house of a great aunt I never heard of called Twill.

I told you my life was pathetic.

# 2

## How Pathetic
## Can You Get?

From the minute I laid eyes on Great Aunt Twill I realized my mother hadn't done her research. The great extremes she had gone to in order to make the best arrangements for me turned out to be a tiny old lady with a pointy nose and hair piled in a cone on top of her head.

She wore an old weathered red velvet cape (yes, *cape*) and big hiking boots, and she looked to be about a hundred years old at least. She showed up while I was eating peanut butter out of the jar with a spoon while watching the cooking channel and learning how to create interesting baking powder biscuits.

"So *you're* Bellflower?!" she boomed. "You look something like your grandmother—that is, your *mother's* mother. But not really. I think you look more like your Great Uncle Zeke—now *he* was a piece of work. I'll tell you about him sometime. Let me look at you. Turn around. Oh never mind. Don't get up. Ah, that's it. You are the spitting image of— *nothing*. Nothing and *nobody*. Get your stuff. We're outta here."

Her face crunched up funny as she looked around the place, and for a second she seemed mad enough to hit something.

Then she opened her arms and came at me. I didn't know what to expect, but I hoped it would be just one of those smothering, rib-crushing hugs grownups like to give children, and not a clobber on the chin. But instead she just patted me on the shoulder and huffed, "Well, come on, let's get this show on the road!"

She saw me hanging onto the peanut butter jar like it was my last earthly friend and her face crunched up again. "Well, bring the peanut butter with you if you must. No sense wasting it."

I put the peanut butter jar and the third-full jar of raspberry jam and the half loaf of Hawaiian sweet bread in a plastic bag from the Cub store and said I was ready to get the show on the road.

"And your things? What about your things? Your clothes, your whatever."

I must have looked dumb.

"Your *things*, Bellflower. Don't you have a suit-case?"

"Why? What for," I asked.

"You'll be *living* with me, that's why," she said. "I can't be buying you everything new, now can I? Do I *look* like I'm made of money?"

I gave a not-so-confident chuckle. "Oh, don't worry. My mother will be back real soon, so no need packing a bunch of stuff." Then I thought for a second. "Well, maybe I should take my toothbrush. My mom's got our suitcase, so I'll just carry my PJs and my Kidz Bible under my arm."

"Oh for goodness sake, try to be civilized," said Great Aunt Twill, "You can't leave here with your things under your arms. That's no way to travel. Pretend you're getting on an airplane instead of riding in my car. Would you carry your clothes draped over your arms, your underwear hanging out of your pockets, your toiletries in your hat? Who'd want to sit next to you?"

She saw the dopey expression on my face and changed her tone.

"OK, Bellflower, OK, OK," she sighed. "I'll come over tomorrow with Lady Mae and we'll pack up your things and clear out the rest of this junk here, not that any of it is worth much."

"Who's Lady Mae?" I asked. (Her Golden Retriever perhaps? Bloodhound? Pit bull?)

"What'd you say?" She was perusing the apartment like somebody shopping for nasty smelling weed control products.

~ 17 ~

"Lady Mae," I said, "Who would that be?"

"Ah, Lady Mae. Lives in my house," said Great Aunt Twill through her teeth. "My sister. Some people call her *Aunt* Lady Mae, even though she's nobody's aunt." She came closer and pointed her finger at my face. "But don't *you*, Bellflower, ever call her aunt."

I could already see this was going to be a real fun experience.

"Actually, Lady Mae is a little peculiar," she went on, "but if you stay out of her way you'll won't get hurt," she said as she kicked the leg of our sofa which Mother bought at the hospice resale with her then fiancé, Lars Lagleby. It was supposed to be *their* sofa after they tied the knot. I didn't like him, like I told you, and I tried to convince my mother she didn't need a fiancé when she had me; after all we were already a family, she and I, but for some reason, she preferred a fiancé. Until she dumped him, that is. She said it was due to the hole in her heart, the one she suffered when she lost my father.

I took another bite of peanut butter and felt a bad case of the hiccups coming on.

# 3

## Welcome to Weirdsville

We arrived at Great Aunt Twill's house in her 1940 Buick (yes, 1940—that's even before Adam and Eve!) and the car was big enough for a family of five to take up residence in. The car didn't go very fast, but the heater worked, and that's what mattered most, she said.

We rattled up to her house—a tall, lopsided thing, shaped like an egg carton on its end with a crooked pointy roof. It was at the end of a long, winding driveway lined with spidery-looking trees. The place didn't look at all friendly, no. It looked more like something the witch in "Hansel and Gretel" lived in.

Great Aunt Twill said my room was upstairs. She ushered me inside and I looked around and didn't see any stairs to my room, so-called. She gave a snort and directed me to a ladder that was propped up in her closet between her mothbally fur coats. The ladder led to an unfinished, dark attic.

She said not to trouble myself about it being so dark up there; she'd string up an extension cord with a lamp so I could see my way around. She said Lady Mae got rid of most of the cobwebs, and they hauled a mattress up there for me to sleep on.

"It's the best we could do, Missy," she told me. "Take it or leave it."

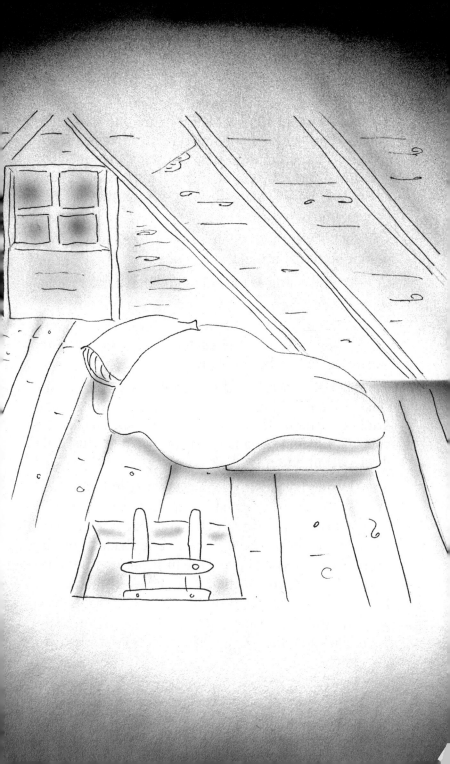

"Thank you," I said, trying to be polite, and wishing my mother could see what she'd gotten me into. Here was her daughter, forced to climb a ladder stuck between a bunch of mothbally coats and then made to sleep in a dark, spidery old attic. This was one weird great aunt, and she didn't disguise the fact that she didn't care much for me.

"Bellflower, is there a reason you're hauling that peanut butter jar around with you?"

"Peanut butter is the only thing that cures my hiccups," I said.

"Oh! You better not be *sick*, my dear. I can't afford to be sending you to the *doctor* every other minute. …Besides, I don't hear any hiccups."

That was because the peanut butter cured me. (This is a good thing for you to remember. Never mind drinking water on the other side of the glass and getting yourself dripping wet and water up your nose. Just gulp down peanut butter.)

On my first night sleeping upstairs in Great Aunt Twill's attic where I hoped the spiders were friendly, I heard noises coming from all the dark corners. I kept the lamp on all night but it cast eerie shadows on the unfinished walls and I could see little pockets of moonlight coming through the cracks between the ceiling beams. The lamplight was hardly bright enough to read by, and the shadows it created against the walls were black looming things like the hugest monsters I ever saw.

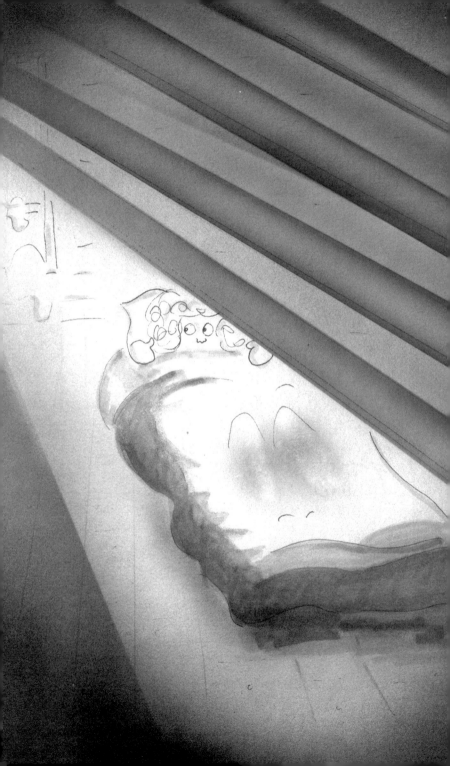

I hoped I would not get eaten by monsters. I prayed a little prayer that in case I got eaten by monsters, God would please watch over my mother and not let her forget me totally.

I wasn't all that good at praying. I learned about praying in my Sunday School class in St. Paul. At first my mother said she didn't want me going to church all by myself. She didn't want me "going all religious" on her, but then she said why not; it was probably better than me hanging around eating peanut butter and watching the cooking channel and being a general pest.

So on Sunday mornings I combed and brushed my hair to make it flat (though it *never* stays flat). I put on my school shoes and clean socks. Then I brushed my teeth twice and put on my one and only dress and waited for the school bus with "God's Chariot" painted on the side to stop in front of our apartment building. The teacher gave us Oreos for snacks which I stuffed in my pockets and ate for two days. And I got a free Kidz Bible.

But back to my pathetic present life: What could the dinky old town of Lake Clearbottom offer a cosmopolitan girl like me who'd already attended more schools than most dogs have fleas? I figured the church in St. Paul had more members than Lake Clearbottom had citizens.

# Places I'd rather live

I believed St. Paul, Minnesota, to be every bit as glamorous as Paris, France, or Rome, Italy, neither of which, I might point out, could boast of an annual Winter Carnival like the one in St. Paul. Besides, St. Paul had a spectacular fireworks show on the 4th of July right in the shadows of the State Capitol building. I loved the food booths, the arts and crafts stuff, the puppet shows, the musical groups, the hordes of people with their kids, and me shouting my head off every time something pretty exploded in the sky.

(I kept the souvenir books in my old bedroom. I am a girl who knows how to maintain historical references.)

"Humph, ain't nothing," groused Great Aunt Twill. The town of Lake Clearbottom had their own carnivals, and could St. Paul ever compare with Lake Clearbottom's annual pork fry festival in January, the heifer jump and harness race in April, or the march of the mud turtles in June?

I didn't know turtles marched.

"That goes to show you," huffed Great Aunt Twill, "how little you cosmopolitan folk know."

I got settled in my freezing cold attic room, and before I had a chance to think any more intelligent thoughts, it was morning and I was on my way to my new school. I had survived the first night.

"Just keep your mouth shut and your nose clean and don't hit anybody," was Great Aunt Twill's school

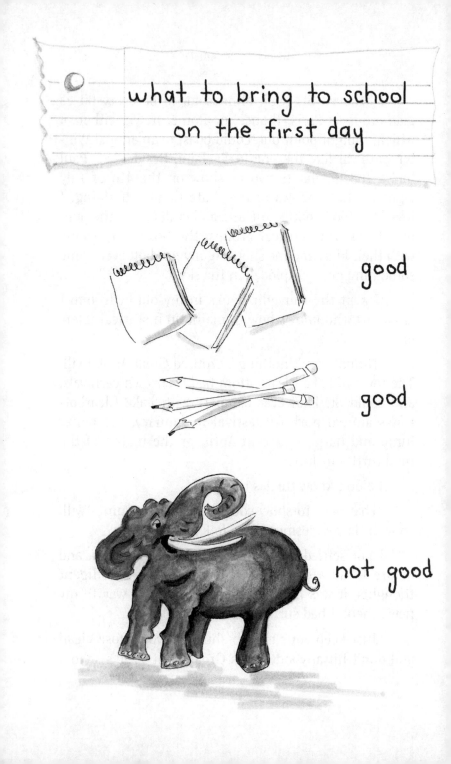

advice. She parked in front of the school (please God, don't let anybody see me getting out of this car) and walked me to the office to register. She strode ahead of me through the halls like a captain leading a soldier to battle.

"Hey no big deal," I said in an assuring voice, "I'm a regular *pro* at starting a new school!"

Once registered and assigned a locker, teacher, and home room, I was whisked off to my classroom, which was a typical classroom, only brighter and newer than most. The textbooks weren't scribbled in and the undersides of desks weren't lumpy with old gum wads. Nobody paid much attention to me. You'd think they got new kids every day.

After school, Great Aunt Twill waited for me at the curb in her embarrassment of a car. She let me know she didn't fancy wasting gas to keep the heater running, and I should hurry up and get my tail out there.

She wasn't alone.

"*This* is Lady Mae," she announced, and I looked into the very round face of a very round woman who looked at me with one eye squinting and her nose wrinkled as though I smelled bad. She fixed her gaze at me and sighed, "So—it's *you*."

I didn't know if that meant hello or go take a hike. I pulled up my shoulders. "You got that right," I said. "It is I."

"Ah! She's a saucy one!" she snapped.

"Well don't just stand there gaping," howled Great Aunt Twill, "get in the dern car."

Lady Mae eyed me with her good eye until we came to the only traffic light in town. "So," she growled, "you're Florence's kid."

"Florence's kid," I said. Florence would be my mother. "Yes," I said. "That I am."

"Well, I wouldn't be so proud of it if I were you."

"You're not me," I said.

Silence. Then Great Aunt Twill busted in with, "So. How was your first day of school?"

I was experienced at answering grownups' dumb questions about school. "Fine," I said. If they asked what subjects I liked best I always answered I liked gym best (or lunch or being late, or whatever I felt like making up. Sometimes I made up a boy's name as my favorite subject, which always got a charming reaction).

"Did you get into any trouble yet?" asked Great Aunt Twill.

Nobody ever asked me *that*. "I don't think so," I said.

"Give her time," said Lady Mae.

I knew right then that Lady Mae and I were in for a very bumpy time of it. Lady Mae outweighed me by about 200 pounds and probably packed a heavy whollop.

We drove up the long driveway to Great Aunt Twill's with the twisting trees doing their snaky dance along each side. She stuck her key in the front door lock, flung open the door and screamed, "We're *home*!" I looked around to see whom she was calling out to.

"Nobody's here." twittered Great Aunt Twill. "I just like to do that." She cast me a testy look. "You got any objections?"

"Nope. Not I. Nosiree" (Yikes. Was the place haunted?)

"All right now, Little Missy, first thing you do after school is your homework. You got homework? Is that a yes?"

(What was with the *Little Missy*?)

"Pay attention! Now here's the schedule: soon as you walk in the house you take ten minutes and you go to the bathroom, you wash your hands, comb that mop on your head, and then you sit yourself down and do your homework. Period. No discussion."

Fine with me. I didn't see a TV or computer anywhere.

"Then it's supper, and after supper, it's dishes, chores, and bed. Got that?"

Chores? Did she say chores? I saw myself hauling hay, gathering eggs, feeding the pony, things I had read about in books. In St. Paul my only duty was frying up some dinner for my mother and me, and it was pretty certain I wasn't going to win any awards in the cooking department.

Great Aunt Twill informed me that my chores would consist of cleaning windows, scrubbing floors, scrubbing walls, scrubbing sinks, pots and pans, sundry fixtures, dusting shelves, washing clothes, polishing furniture, polishing silver and brass, and other small household chores.

"Work builds character, I say," she said with a wobbly smile.

The air in the bathroom was as cold as the air in the attic. An electric heater stood under the sink, and Great Aunt Twill explained it was to be used only for bath time.

"A little brisk air never hurt anyone," she said. "It builds character."

I closed the door and sat on the edge of the bathtub which was parked in the middle of the room. I had never seen a bathtub parked in the middle of a room, and I had never seen such a huge bathroom. It was as big as my bedroom in our apartment in St. Paul.

The floor in the bathroom was marble tile and the ceiling seemed a mile up overhead. Pale, thin towels hung from hooks on the wall, and one small braided rug lay in front of the sink. I looked out the window at the empty landscape. Flat, dreary land layered with dead, brown grass. Black outlines of trees with clumps of dead leaves hanging from their branches. A grey winter sky.

It was a fitting background for a TV documentary on manic depression.

"What on earth are you doing in there, Bellflower? It's time for your homework!" Lady Mae yelled through the door.

"Just combing my mop," I called back. I used Great Aunt Twill's silver hairbrush (it needed polishing) from the carved oak stand that the sink sat on. The sink wasn't a sink, really, more like a bowl. A wash bowl, I guess you'd call it. And a mop I guess you'd call my hair. My mother said I didn't get my hair from *her*. *Her* hair was long and silky and prettiness. Mine was, well, frizz and mess and madness.

My books, a new notebook, two sharpened pencils, and a ballpoint pen waited for me on the kitchen table, along with a bowl of marshmallows.

"I don't do cookies," said Great Aunt Twill.

# 4

## Don't Hate Me
## Because I'm Smart

Lady Mae parked herself on a kitchen chair to keep an eye on me. She glared at me with her one good eye and worked her mouth as if chewing on something.

I asked Great Aunt Twill if I might have a bit of peanut butter to go with the marshmallows, and she set the jar down on the table with a clunk. "Don't ask for milk. I don't do milk."

Long pause. "...How about a cup of coffee?" she said.

"Sure," I said, like I drank coffee every day.

"Black?"

"What other colors have you got?"

Lady Mae let out a snort. Great Aunt Twill brought out a cup. "Like I *said*, I don't do *milk*, and I also don't do cream. Maybe you'd prefer Ovaltine."

"What's that?"

"Didn't your mother ever give you Ovaltine?"

I shook my head, no. I was watching Lady Mae who was chomping away on nothing.

"How about bugleaid? Did she ever give you a glass of lemon water with a dash of bitters and a rind of mango and pineapple? I call it bugleaid."

"Oh sure," I said. "All the time."

"HAR!" laughed Lady Mae, and with her mouth wide open I swear I saw a cavern of black goop inside.

"Makes you feel like blowing a bugle, that's why I call it bugleaid. Like lemonade, only bugleaid. But since you drink it all the time, you know all about that."

I opened my science book. I was supposed to draw a diagram about the layers of dirt on the earth. The rest of the class had already drawn their diagrams, but I could catch up with them in no time. I was good at diagrams, even though English was my ultimate best subject.

I read out loud, "Plants and weather create dirt. The first living things on earth were plants and they grew out of the water on top of the rocks and then with the help of wind and rain, the roots of the plants broke the rocks and then the plants died, and so crumbled rock and dead plants make dirt." I closed the book. "There you have it."

"Whatzat?" said Great Aunt Twill.

"Dirt," I said.

"Dirt," laughed Lady Mae with another "*Har.*"

"The earth is always changing," I explained. "Small changes make big changes. Wind and water grind down mountains. Ice digs out holes that later fill with water to become lakes. Like Lake Clearbottom."

Lady Mae stared at me with wonder all over her chubby face. "You *like* book learning, Missy?"

Missy again. I drew a circle on my paper showing the crust of the earth, its mantle, its liquid core, and its solid core. I wondered where my own crayons and colored pencils were. "Books open the doors and windows of the universe to little eyes," I said with a smug smile, quoting the exact words of one of my fifth grade teachers.

"Well, don't that beat all," whuffed Lady Mae.

"I don't trust her," said Great Aunt Twill, "but she got it right what she said about ice." (She was still thinking about how ice creates holes that fill with water that form lakes, if you follow me.)

"Come winter, Lake Clearbottom is one big block of ice," said Great Aunt Twill. "Solid ice! The men in town set up little shacks out in the middle of the lake, and they sits inside and waits for the fish to bite. To this day I can't figure out why men would want to do such a dern thing. You don't see a group of *gals* hightailing themselves out in 30-below-zero weather with a 70-below wind-chill factor to sit over a hole in the ice all night waiting for a dern fish to bite, now do you?"

Lady Mae gave a cough and I swear I saw something black string out of the side of her mouth. (What *was* that yucky stuff? My curiosity nearly cost me my little toe, but more about that later.)

"Listen here, Bellflower," said Great Aunt Twill, "we drove over to St. Paul to your apartment today while you were in school, Lady Mae and I, and we packed up all what was possible and hauled it over here. Your mother asked if I'd put her sorry furniture in storage, so it's stored down in my basement, thanks to my generous nature."

"My mother will be back soon," I said, "to take it all off your hands."

"Don't hold your breath, dearie. You can cart your own things up to the attic yourself. I'm not as young as I used to be. And Lady Mae here nearly got herself a crick in her neck wiping down all those spider webs. Not to mention her sore back from hauling that there mattress up the ladder."

Lady Mae gave a sniff.

"Did you bring my rock collection?"

"That was a *collection*? My stars, I thought it was the dern town dump."

"And what about my tile chips?" I said.

"Tile chips?"

"*My collection of tile chips.* I've been saving them for ages. I save pieces of broken tile, see, and some day I'm going to make a mosaic wall."

"Bellflower, most little girls your age collect dolls and purses. Why don't you collect dolls and purses like most other little girls?"

"I'm not a little girl. I'm eleven years old, practically a teenager."

"Eleven going on thirty-five," chortled Lady Mae, and she rolled out of her chair and began to prepare supper. I hurried out of the kitchen to check on my stuff.

What a relief to find Great Aunt Twill hadn't tossed my rocks and precious tile chips. They were in a pillow case with some sand and a half dead philodendron plant. Living with these two old ladies wasn't going to be a picnic. Oh well, it would just be for a little while.

Personal Private KEEP OUT this means YOU Journal

Dear Mother:
Today I got an A on my drawing of the layers of the earth. You are further away from me than 20 miles, and the part of the earth we live on is the crust and it's about 20 miles thick. So a big "Hi and Hello" from this side of the

crust. Did you ~~know~~ Know that if you put a grain of sand on a peach it would stick up more on the peach than the highest mountain does on this earth ?? Just thought you'd like to Know.

The atmosphere around the earth is changing. So beware.

Your daughter,

Bellflower Munch

# 5

## More Un-Fun
## in Lake Clearbottom

Wintertime in Lake Clearbottom was nothing like wintertime in the big city of St. Paul, let me tell you.

In the big city I crunched around on the sidewalks lathered in salt and wrecked my boots when they got all white and crusty. In Lake Clearbottom they don't salt the sidewalks. I slide and crunch around on *clean* snow.

In the city I saw the Christmas lights from every window of our apartment and I heard the racket of traffic on the nearby freeway. In Lake Clearbottom it is as quiet as the inside of a moth's cocoon.

In the big city there were *thieves* and *panhandlers, pickpockets* and *bank robbers* running around left and right! What does the town of Lake Clearbottom have? Silent fields of white snow, bare trees, a town with one main street, one traffic light, and a frozen lake.

However, one thing the big city did not have and the town of Lake Clearbottom does have, is Great Aunt Twill. She was never without her *cape*. I wondered if she had a broom hidden somewhere out on the yard that she hopped on when no one was watching. Some days she wore a blue cape and some days red. But she *always* wore a cape, and she also always wore her big, heavy hiking boots. She was one of a kind, you might say.

But on Sundays Great Aunt Twill got dressed up. She wore a purple cape with white polka dots and flamenco dancing shoes. (Right. Flamenco dancing shoes, as in Spanish click-clickety-click-click.)

Lady Mae, on the other hand, always wore a big cotton house dress and men's slippers. She was the only person I ever met who didn't need a coat in the winter. She said she had body padding to keep her warm. She pranced along in the winter air wearing her soft cotton house dress, and if there was snow on the ground she pulled on a pair of high black rubber boots over her slippers and was good to go.

"Just be glad it's not summer and you're not slapping at chiggers and mosquitoes day and night," she exclaimed trudging through the snow in her big boots.

"My mother will come for me before Christmas," I told them.

Tipping her head down, Great Aunt Twill looked at me over the top of her eyeglasses and gave a loud snort.

"Well, I think she *will*," I said with conviction. "She'll be here all right."

Great Aunt Twill grunted, "Christmas is not that far off. Don't get your hopes up."

Great Aunt Twill called the living room the "parlor," and it was the only room she kept heated. It's where they spent most of their time except for eating meals in the kitchen where the stove gave off enough heat to keep them from getting frost bite. "The brisk winter air builds character," she explained.

The sun had set and a light snow began to fall. Great Aunt Twill busied herself writing her annual Christmas letter in the parlor while I sat on the floor by the piano that didn't work, but I had polished to a gleaming glory. I sat there trying to remember how many Christmas songs I could sing by heart.

"HARK, THE HAROLD ANGELS SI-ING," I crowed. Then I said to Great Aunt Twill, "What's a *harold* angel?"

"*Herald* angels *herald* things," she said, annoyed at the interruption. "Like when the angels heralded the birth of Christ."

"Ah."

She went back to writing her Christmas letter, which, I found out, she never bothers to mail to anyone. She wrote about interesting events of life throughout the year, like when she began taking her flamenco dance classes, and when she added periwinkle wallpaper to the front hall. In September she got the back porch painted a blushing rose color, and mercy me, it's December already.

"What's *hark*?"

"Goodness, Bellflower! I'm concentrating! Are you ten years old and don't know the meaning of *hark*?"

"Eleven."

"Whatever. Ten, eleven, forty-two, it's all the same to me. Hark means listen. It means pay attention."

I started the song again. *"Hark the harold angels si-ing, glory to the newborn King!" Peace on earth and mercy mi-ld..."*

"Do you mind keeping it down?" said Great Aunt Twill.

I could take a hint. I jumped on one foot to the closet and climbed the ladder to the attic. The attic smelled like old wood and the cold didn't help. Nobody ever thought to put heating ducts in the attic because I suppose nobody ever thought someone would be living up there, namely me. In the daytime, the sun shone through the cracks between the roof and the wall beams, and I could almost always see dust floating in the air.

The attic was a good place for singing loud. Up there I could sing to my heart's content and entertain the mice and the spiders. The attic was also good for writing in my *Personal Private Keep Out This Means YOU* journal (after I figured out how to hold a pen wearing mittens).

I began chipping off the ice and snow from the attic window so I could see outside. I pecked a hole with the pen and could see the snow-covered trees and the small, silver tail of Lake Clearbottom beyond the rooftops of the houses. Maybe if I looked hard enough I could see my old apartment house in St. Paul.

I wondered if anybody in this world missed me.

# 6

## Poem Trouble

Three weeks at Lake Clearbottom Middle School and I made a friend! His name was Skoot Bittle and he was in the sixth grade like me, except he was in Section One. It's hard to believe in a small town like Lake Clearbottom that we'd have two sixth grades; but kids were bussed from all over the place, and each classroom was jammed full. For some reason the sixth grade exploded with kids. I liked Skoot right off. He could spit through his front teeth and recite the Star Spangled Banner backward. A real talent.

The complete history of marshmallows

Skoot also liked marshmallow sandwiches, which is what my Great Aunt Twill packed in my lunch box. No matter how many times I offered to pack my own lunch,

Great Aunt Twill refused, and insisted on taking control of the refrigerator and all that was therein, and would Lady Mae please pass the pickles? (She always included a fat, juicy dill pickle in my lunch which got the marshmallow sandwich soggy. We're talking real taste thrills here.)

Skoot was the only person who said, "yum" when he saw my marshmallow sandwiches and pickles, instead of "yuk!" and shivering like all the dweeby girls. We usually traded and I got a cheese bagel for my marshmallow sandwich.

Our teacher, Miss Kreek, gave us a poem assignment. We were supposed to write a poem about something that made us glad.

Glad? Was she serious? I had to think hard on that one.

"You any good at poems?" Skoot asked me while munching on a pickle.

"Sure. At my last school they called me Sylvia Plath Longfellow."

He looked confused. "Who?"

"Great poets, that's who."

"Would you help me with my poem?" he wanted to know. "All I can come up with is just three little old lines."

"Oh. Like a haiku," I said.

"A what?"

"A haiku, you know, a three-line poem of 17 syllables. When I was in the 4th grade I went to one school for almost five months and I had this teacher who just came back from Japan and everything we did was Japanese. From haiku to origami to chopsticks and sushi. I won the haiku contest but we moved again before the day the awards were handed out..."

"Bellflower," Scoot said, "this is urgent. Can you help me? Listen:

*When I think of something that makes me glad*

*I think of my dog who is never sad.*

*He's so much fun and so good, too...*

He stopped and scratched his ear. "What rhymes with too? —Oh, OK, I got it. How's this:

*Such a good dog like mine I wish for you.*"

"You're right. You need help," I said. Then I had an idea. I asked Skoot about what made him glad: "Finding trouble and solving it, soccer, baseball, swimming, and my dog," he added. His big, drooling, goofy dog, of which breed he was not certain.

I made a note, worked some words around and handed him this:

### GLAD

A soccer ball in the corner of my room,

my baseball mitt hanging in the garage,

my swim goggles and Junior's leash in my hand,

and all I need is summer.

(I told you I was good in English. I'm a regular Shakespeare.)

Skoot looked at me like I just dropped down from another planet.

"You call that a poem?"

"Why not? Ever read Petrarch? Milton? Walt Whitman? They all had to start somewhere."

"Have you read all those guys?"

"Sure," I lied, "hasn't everyone?"

"Okay, Smartie," he said, "But my dog's name isn't Junior."

"No?"

"No. It's *Rabbit*."

(A dog named Rabbit. So what's the cat's name? Rhinoceros?)

I changed the subject. "Skoot, do you want to hear about the school where I got into poem trouble?"

"Poem trouble?" Skoot was immediately interested. Skoot loved trouble because, as I would soon find out, Lake Clearbottom was loaded with trouble. I'd also found out that Skoot was a regular top notch sleuth (*sleuth:* hot shot detective, my definition). Skoot was a crazed sleuth when it came to trouble. He had a real *gift* for trouble, you might say.

"Well, here's how it went down," I said. "See, I had this teacher in Minneapolis who wrote poetry and she even had a book published. So she had us writing a poem a day, short ones, you know, to express our moods and our innermost feelings. The only one rule she had: *no rhyming.*"

"Is this the same teacher who traveled to Japan?"

"No. This is another one."

I paused to chuckle remembering the commotion my poems caused.

"I wrote a poem about murdering my mother's at-the-time boyfriend."

"Murder? Did you say *murder*?"

"Yeah, I wrote about a plan to murder my mother's fiancé, who was one big phony, let me tell you. It was him or me. Anyhow, I wrote about setting fire to his hat with him in it. Ha-ha!"

Skoot shot up from his chair.

"With him in it," I repeated, for emphasis.

"No kidding," said Skoot. "That's *awful.*"

"Sure is, was. Really awful." I gave out a big sigh. "Well, gotta run. Ta-ta," I said, and left him sitting in the lunch room with his eyes bulging out of his head (obviously unacquainted with the conventions of fiction.)

After school I took my sweet time putting my things in my backpack because I knew Lady Mae and Great Aunt Twill would be waiting for me all growly faced and snooty. I was in no hurry to see either one of them.

Skoot met me in the hall.

"Hey," he said.

"Hey yourself," I said.

"Guess what. My teacher liked the poem, so-called. Thought you'd like to know. She said it was, well, original."

I gave him a shrug.

"Hey, Bellflower, want to go ice skating?"

"Right now?" (Heck, I'd go bungee jumping with wild crocodiles right now if he asked me.)

I told him sure, why not, "but I warn you," I said as honest as I could, "I've never ice skated in my life."

"Never?"

"Never."

"Okay, you can borrow my sister's skates. She won't mind."

"Deal. Come on, we'll give you a ride home," I said. I figured if we gave Skoot a ride, Lady Mae might ignore me.

"Ride in *that* car? Wow! Sure!" He actually seemed excited about getting inside Great Aunt Twill's car. Skoot knew right away where Great Aunt Twill's house was–small town, you know, everybody knows where everybody else lives.

Walking toward the car I said we could have some marshmallows and bugleaid at Great Aunt Twill's house.

The color left his face. His eyes bugged out and he started twitching.

"*What?*"

"Well," he started, "it's just that—I don't think your aunts like kids—exactly."

I laughed out loud and gave him a poke in the rib. "What else is new?"

# 7

## Fate Strikes on the Rink

"What's bugleaid? Poison?" He cracked up laughing.

"Very funny, Skoot. I'll have you know, bugleaid happens to be an *exotic* beverage from *ancient times*—not exactly a lie; isn't Great Aunt Twill what you'd call ancient? Bugleaid is from a secret recipe, so secret that only a very few chosen ones know about it. The secret recipe is kept in a secret vault (yeah, right, Great Aunt Twill's head) and available to no one on the face of the earth except a very chosen few (that would be me and Lady Mae, I suppose). I drink it with great reverence, for with each sip I feel I am swallowing a bit of history."

I had his complete attention.

"Wow! You mean it's some sort of drink like from Egypt or something? Like what they drank in ancient days?"

(I amaze myself.) "You got it, Sherlock," I said. He was all questions as he followed me to Great Aunt Twill's car. He piled in next to me and I was so right about Lady Mae ignoring me with Skoot in the car. She turned into a regular chief of police asking him stuff. She wanted to know about his father, what his father was doing, where his father worked, how many years had he been married to his mother, how old was his sister, did his father go to any school reunions…blah, blah, blah.

Skoot whispered to me he'd come in for bugleaid some other time. He asked Great Aunt Twill if I could go ice skating with him, and said I could borrow his sister's skates.

Great Aunt Twill let out a screech. "ICE SKATING! Bellflower, are you trying to give me a heart attack? Listen here, I can't be footing any hospital bills. I'm no *nurse* either. *Got that*?! Don't you come running to *me* when you break a leg!"

I looked at Skoot's face which had turned pink and I started to laugh.

"What's so gosh dern funny?" said Great Aunt Twill.

"You are," I said, being my almost-honest self, but I couldn't help wonder why Skoot looked so scared.

A rink had been cleared of snow on the frozen lake and when Skoot and I got there, it was already crowded with people ice skating. Old people, young people, kids—you'd think someone was handing out money, it was so crowded.

Skating away was the owner of the dry cleaning store, who went by the initials, A.R., and his big standard poodle, who didn't actually skate, but kept his eye on A.R. There was the postman, Mr. Pettlefry, and my teacher, Miss Kreek, and almost everybody else in the town of Lake Clearbottom. Being here over a month, I pretty much knew who everyone was in the entire town.

We changed into our skates in the warming house where there were benches along the walls and a big gas stove in the center. The room was hot and smelled of wet wool and feet. I laced up Skoot's sister's ice skates and headed out the door for the ice like I knew what I was doing.

"Hey, not so fast!" Skoot called after me.

Too late. I was already zinging down the path to the ice, and then I was hurdling across the ice, my arms flapping at my sides, my eyes stinging in the wind. It would have been fun if I could have figured out how to stop myself.

I went flying to one end of the rink, hit the fence, bounced back onto the ice and went spinning until I fell flat on my backside. Skoot skated up to me laughing, and so did three or four other kids

from my class at school, one of them being Arnold Arkvard, my Number 1 Most Un-favorite Person.

"Wow, Bellflower. That was really stupid." (Arnold Arkvard made fun of my hair the second day of school. He took one look at the mass confusion called hair on my head and he yelled out, "Garbage-Head!" I'd get him for that.)

We skated, or I should say everyone else skated, and I scuttled around the ice hanging onto the fence for dear life.

I was glad when I saw Arnold Arkvard leave with his friends because then I could concentrate on happier thoughts. One thing I discovered as I watched the

ice skaters, is that the people seemed much happier on the ice than on dry ground. When they were twirling around on the ice and winging through the air on thin little blades, the world to them must have appeared to be a very pleasant, congenial place. They seemed to have not a care in the world when flinging around on the ice. I wouldn't know—my backside hurt and my feet got cold real fast.

"See that kid over there going into the warming house?" Skoot nodded toward a skinny kid our age wearing a red Santa hat and matching mittens.

I nodded, trying to stand upright on the skates without my ankles caving in.

"That's Martin Menkin. He's got real bad asthma. The kind where you're allergic to everything under the sun, even air."

The boy disappeared into the warming house. "But he can't be that sick. He skates better than I do."

"*Everyone* skates better than *you* do," Skoot huffed. He gave me a smile to show he was joking, except he wasn't joking. I was terrible at ice skating.

"I think it's time for me to go home," I told him. My feet were so cold I was sure when I got the skates off my feet I'd find two cakes of ice with toes.

Skoot helped me stumble into the warming house where we took off our skates and put on our

shoes. I smiled at Martin Menkin, the kid with the bad asthma. "Hi Marty! I'm Bellflower," I said, introducing myself. "I'm new here."

"Good for you," he said.

"Yuppers, good for me," I said, unfazed by his rudeness. "Hey, I saw you out there on the ice. Wow, you're really terrific. Where'd you learn to skate like that?"

"Thanks," he said in a flat voice.

"I could watch you all day," I rattled on, "You make it look like so much fun, so easy! Me, I can hardly stand up on those iddy biddy blades without seriously pulling something out of joint. But *you*—I mean, I felt like applauding!"

He swung his skates over his shoulder. "Bye," he said.

I watched him leave with a funny feeling in the bottom of my stomach. Rude, yes. Unfriendly, absolutely. Still, I couldn't help feeling there was something special about him.

"He always keeps to himself," Skoot said. "His parents were supposed to have been professional ice skaters, that is, until his dad left them."

My heart gave a clunk. "*Left* them?"

"Left them as in *divorce*, not as in left them *to run off to California*."

"Ah."

He looked uneasy, like there was more to the story.

"So what else?" I said, trying not to think about my mother leaving me to find her authentic self.

"It's just that, well, he had a twin sister. And well, she's gone missing."

I got a breath caught in my larynx or my esophagus, and I started to choke.

"She's gone missing and nobody even talks about it," he continued. "She was in our class at school. Very quiet and unfriendly, that one. Like Martin. By the way, he likes to be called Martin, not Marty."

That night in the attic shivering on my mattress on the floor, I tried to be thankful that I didn't have asthma.

An entry in my *Personal Private Keep Out This Means YOU* journal:

Personal Private **KEEP OUT** this means
**YOU** Journal

WHAt MaKes Me Glad

NOT MUCH
and that is saying
a lot.
— a non- haiku
by Bellflower Munch

After I stared out the window for about ten hours, I wrote a letter to Jesus. I stuck it in my *Personal Private Keep Out This Means YOU* journal.

Dear Jesus, my mother would be so sad if her daughter had a bad case of asthma. Please watch over her and tell her not to worry about me because I'm a perfectly healthy girl who does not have asthma, which I just learned how to spell. It's a word I don't like and I'm going to put it on my "Remove From Dictionary" list.

Bellflower's Words to Remove from the Dictionary

MATH

HoMe WorK (MATH)

Orphan

ASTHMA

# 8

## Harold Shows Up

At the bottom of my poem paper Miss Kreek put a big "See Me." Which I did. See her. "You could do better," she told me, removing her glasses. (I was in for a lecture, I could tell. When the glasses come off, it's lecture time.)

She started out saying something about some potential down inside me if I just tried a little harder. Then came the complaint about my "attitude." I was used to this. Every teacher I ever met had a talk to me about my "attitude."

No problem. I dove right into my Poor Bellflower act. "Gosh, you're right about my bad attitude," I sniffed. "I must try a little harder." I said this with the pathetic look on my face which I used to make teachers feel ashamed they aren't nicer to me.

When Miss Craven, one of my fifth grade teachers, called me up to her desk to talk about my *attitude*, I burst into a flood of tears with a dramatic rush of apologies and explanations about how my mother worked nights, and it was so terribly lonely, and how all alone and scared I was at night. That was the best. She felt so sorry for me that she bought me lunch.

My performance wasn't working with Miss Kreek, though. She watched me with a bored expression. In fact, she looked like she might start snoring. "Be that as it may," she said after I practically threw myself on the floor wailing. "Bellflower, you're behind in math."

Math. Why, oh why, do we have to learn math?

"Pay attention, Bellflower," Miss Kreek went on. "I'll give you one week to make up your work," she said. "As for English, write me a better poem. One with stanzas."

Apparently she didn't realize English was my strong subject and that I could be quite the little poet if I set my mind to it. I gave a shrug and worked my neck down into my collar, which made my cheeks bulge out and my face turn crimson.

Miss Kreek gave a start. "Stop that!" she gasped. "Young lady, you *must* work on your *attitude*! You're a smart and creative girl, but it won't help you in life to be smart and creative if you have a bad attitude, you know. What would your *father* say?"

My father? What ever made her mention my father? My father died before I was born and every time I asked my mother about him, she got so upset we had to change the subject. She simply refused to talk about him except to tell me what a great guy he was, and he was too young to die. She didn't want to talk about the past and that was that. Period. Sometimes I worried

# Exciting careers not requiring MATH

Gorilla keeper at zoo

Ballet star starring the great Bellflowerina

Rich princess spinning gold while waiting for Rumpelstiltskin

I FEEL AN ODE IN THE AIR— AND NO MATH!

Pulitzer poet living off the land

about coming down with the same awful disease and die young, too.

Now here was Miss Kreek asking me about my *father*. "He's dead," I told her with the saddest face I could muster up.

Her expression changed immediately. "Oh, my dear," she said. "Oh, my dear."

I hoped from now on she'd leave me alone about my *attitude*. I sulked all the way home in the Buick thinking about all the mysteries of life that eluded me— and the math homework I still had to make up. (Math. Why do you suppose they ever invented math?)

When we arrived back at Great Aunt Twill's, there was a letter waiting for me from my mother. I threw my backpack on the floor and waved the letter in front of Great Aunt Twill's nose. "See? See? I *told* you!" I chirped. "I told you I wouldn't be staying here long. "I've got a letter from my *mother*. She'll be coming for me soon. I *told* you!"

I wouldn't have to do that math make-up work for Miss Kreek after all. Ha! I'd be in a new school in no time. I'd be starting all over again. Yay! I hurried up the ladder to my attic room to read the letter. I was so excited, I fumbled the envelope and dropped it twice, but I finally got it open and read:

*Dear Bellflower:*

*Please don't send me any more dead spiders.*
*I believe you when you say there are bugs in*

*Great Aunt Twill's attic. Please try to be good. I got a part-time job today selling dresses since my cosmetician license is bogus in California. These California women buy dresses like hot cakes and I'm on commission. Big kiss.*

*Love, Mother*

*P.S. Buy some insect spray!*

When I crawled into bed that night, I felt colder than ever. I thought this could be the night I'd freeze right to death. I wondered if my mother had considered the fact that one day I'd wake up frozen right to death. There I was, freezing under my blanket hoping spiders wouldn't crawl on me during the night. And what if there were mice? I figured if there were mice, they were probably hungry. Maybe an 11-year-old girl would be just the supper they dreamed of all their hairy little lives, probably.

I was feeling plenty nervous when I heard a noise, not like the creaking, mousy noises I heard in the rafters, but another kind of noise—like a heart beat. I stayed quiet and listened. Then I heard the noise again. The room was suddenly brighter, like someone flashed sunlight on everything. I gasped and hugged my pillow tight. I wished I had my old teddy bear from before my mother decided I was too old for teddy bears and gave my Johnny Panda Bear to the trash man to take away.

I held my breath. Great Aunt Twill said sometimes sewer rats came up through the walls from the cellar. Sewer rats!

I shot up to a seated position and began singing the one song I remembered from Sunday school. *"Jesus loves me, this I know..."*

Sewer rats were nasty creatures, Lady Mae relished telling me, they ate babies right in their cribs.

"*...for the Bible tells me so...*"

My voice was shaky. "...Great Aunt Twill, is that...you?"

No answer.

"*...Little ones to Him belong*—Lady Mae, are you playing tricks on me?"

Then a strange sort of silence filled the attic. Everything was quiet. I couldn't even hear the wind blowing outside.

And what happened next was a total *shock*!

All at once the entire attic was washed in light, a soft glowing sort of light. But not like from a light switch light, this light actually hummed. And out of the light came a voice.

A voice!

"Hello, Bellflower," said the voice.

I pressed my eyes shut. Was I dreaming?

"Don't be afraid," said the voice.

Oh sure. A blinding light speaks to me in the dead of night in the attic and I should be *calm*?!

"Open your eyes, Bellflower. I'm a messenger from Heaven," said the voice.

It felt like two bricks were on my eyelids...but I opened them. A messenger from Heaven? Hello?

"The Lord has sent me to you," said the voice.

Squinting my eyes in the brightness I could make out the shape of someone standing in front of me. Whoever it was, was taller than the beams of the attic and it didn't seem to matter. He went right through the beams, the walls, the roof.

"The Lord sent you?" I said. You mean the *Lord* Lord?"

"Yes. I am an angel of the Lord God," said the figure in front of me. "He has given me permission to come to you."

The attic was now completely filled with light. I wasn't cold—suddenly everything felt warm and welcoming. I squinted harder. If this was a dream, it was a nice dream and I didn't want it to go away.

I could make out the figure better now. I saw arms, a face…maybe I should do something like bow, or cross myself, or fall face-down on the floor. I tried to kneel, but my foot got caught in my jacket and I toppled over with a thud.

"Oh no, don't do that," the angel protested. "You must kneel only to the Lord God and Jesus, His Son. I am just an angel. I am just one of God's servants."

I rubbed my eyes. I couldn't find my voice to say something. What I wanted to say was, "You mean you're really an angel? Like from *God*? From *God* God? Are you really and truly a *good* angel from *God in Heaven*?"

The angel seemed to understand what I was thinking.

"I am God's angel," he said. "I've been sent by God. From God in Heaven."

I tried to swallow, catch my breath. What could I do? "What do you want me to do?" I blurted.

"Just be yourself," said the angel. "You are greatly loved just for yourself. The Lord Jesus loves you with a love that will never end or wear out."

I could have fainted right there, but I'm not the type. (When I was in third grade I knew this girl who fainted all the time. Every time something went wrong, bingo, over she went. At the time I thought that was so cool.) Now here I was, in my woolly pajamas and winter jacket talking with an angel whose light was bright enough to light up the whole town. Fainting would not be cool.

"Bellflower, the Lord Jesus wants you to trust Him."

He called me Bellflower, my real name. He didn't call me Bell or Flower or Dumb Head, he called me Bellflower.

"Oh. OK," I said. "*Yes*. Yes, I *will* trust the Lord."

Everything was beautiful at that moment, the sky, the attic, me, life, everything.

I took in a deep breath. "Mr. Angel sir—your angel-ship—um, you know my name, but what do...I call you?"

"What would you like to call me?" said the angel. He smiled and then, of all things, he sat down beside me on the edge of the bed! (Tell me I'm not dreaming.)

"…Well, aren't all angels called Harold? You know, as in *Hark the Harold Angels Sing*?"

"Call me Harold," said the beautiful, shining angel.

He smiled again and everything in me smiled back. My toes smiled. My fingernails smiled. My eyelashes smiled. My belly button smiled. All of me turned into one humungous smile.

How many times in a kid's life does one sit on a mattress in the attic chatting with an *angel* from Heaven!?

"Bellflower," said the angel, "do you remember the day you prayed and gave your life to the Lord Jesus?"

"I think so," I answered. "It was in Sunday School. I was nine and a half, going on ten."

"All of Heaven rejoiced over you that day," said Harold. "And the Lord sent the Holy Spirit to live in your heart the minute you prayed."

I had asked Jesus to make me His child even though I was nine and a half, going on ten at the time and hardly a *child*.

"Bellflower, the Lord wants you to know more about Him and His Kingdom here on earth."

His Kingdom here on earth? Did this mean I'd be moving again?

"God will speak to you in many ways. He especially wants to speak to you by His written Word. His written words are alive, just as He is alive."

Written Word. That means Bible. I hadn't seen my Bible since I arrived at Great Aunt Twill's.

"God has many things to tell you and teach you, dear one. I've been summoned to help you, but before I can help you any more, you must pray and spend more time alone with God."

I shook my head vigorously, yes, yes. Alone with God. OK.

"Talk to Him every single day, Bellflower. He loves your prayers."

(Just tonight I had prayed I wouldn't get eaten by mice.)

"He knows about that, too," said Harold chuckling. "God knows all things because He is omnipotent, omniscient, and omnipresent."

"I'm afraid I don't know what those words mean," I said, even though I was no stranger to the dictionary.

"They mean," said Harold, "God is all powerful. He's everywhere at once. And He knows all things."

"Does He love *every*body?"

"Yes," said Harold. "He loves the whole world. But sadly, not everyone loves Him back."

I remembered another song they sang in Sunday School about loving God better every day and I tried to sing it. Harold sang along with me.

"Lovely," said Harold. "Do you mean it?"

I started to answer him, but in order to be really honest, I had to think about it because a person wouldn't *dare* lie to an angel. Did I love the Lord better every day? Some days I hardly gave Him a thought!

Harold leaned closer to me. "The Lord wants you to activate your gifts, dear. His Holy Spirit will help you."

"Who, me? Gifts? Activate? Huh?"

"Yes, you. Yes, gifts. Your heavenly Father has given you many gifts. Your calling is to be a great blessing to others."

Me a blessing? Me?

I shivered. It was a strange, happy shiver. I didn't say anything; I just sat there grinning like an idiot. Like this was a hot summer afternoon and I was having the best time of my life playing on the beach with God's angel, Harold.

Except now Harold was starting to fade. "Hey, you're not leaving, are you?" The light grew softer and dimmer. I wanted to jump up and protest when I saw Harold begin to fade, but instead, I could only smile and whisper thanks—and from my whole heart, I meant it.

Remember,
Bellflower...

"Remember all that I've told you. Remember it all, Bellflower," he whispered, and he left me.

I sat in the darkness for a long time. I waited for the cold air to sweep across the attic again, but it stayed warm! Harold was gone but I was still toasty warm. Sitting there in the quiet I thought of a million questions I should have asked. Why didn't I ask the questions when he was here? Questions like, can God hear my thoughts? Why did He make spiders? And, what does it mean to *activate my gifts?*

I decided to pray. I knelt on the mattress and began by asking the Lord to forgive my sins. (I named every sin I could think of for the Lord to forgive.) I felt sad and sorry if I had disappointed Him—after all, I was a girl with an *attitude*.

I told the Lord I wanted to make Him happy. If I did what Harold told me to do maybe I could make God happy probably. I climbed under my blanket, and still didn't feel a bit cold. That night I didn't shiver or shake or even need my jacket or mittens.

Wait a second. A thought struck me. Was Harold's visit a *warning*? Did he show up just to prepare me for something terrible about to happen? Yikes! Was the dreaded ax of fate about to fall on me? Was I in for something awful?

*Oh, don't think about that now, Bellflower. Try to go to sleep.*

I rolled over to my side and saw the moon outside the window through the frost. There it was, like a rigid ax of ice ready to fall.

# 9

## Great Aunt Twill's
## Deep, Dark Secrets

During the night, snow had piled up on the window ledge and it was blowing across the attic floor when I woke up. I realized for sure I didn't dream about Harold the angel because the air was still warm, and that was impossible.

(I remembered a verse in the Bible that says, "nothing is impossible with God," and that meant I was a living, breathing miracle because it wasn't cold in the attic even though there was snow on the floor!) I sat up on my mattress and looked for my mittens. But my hands felt toasty warm! And so did my nose, which was *always* cold in the mornings.

OK, let me get this straight. God sent an angel with a message for me from the Lord Jesus. It wasn't every day an angel came dancing into the attic to have a few words, now was it? He said I'm supposed to start reading my Bible more, and not just on Sundays, wasn't that what he said? And didn't he say that God wanted to hear from me?

That meant prayer!

I knelt on my mattress to show I could be an obedient girl. I'd even mention my attitude, and ask Him to help me change.

Personal Private KEEP OUT this means YOU journal

Dear Lord Jesus,

I don't feel worthy of a visit from heaven. In fact, I am probably the least person to hear from an angel. Connie ~~Conklin~~ McConklin in my class at school, now she's really worthy. She washes her hair 4 times a week, and she gets straight A's in absolutely everything, including MATH. Ms. Kreek is ~~always~~ always saying we should all be more like Connie McConklin. Me— well, what can I say? Am I bad?

Was I ~~bad~~ to spit on Gregory Trailbender's fruit loops today? And remember when I sucked all the salt off Sady Mae's Dorito chips and then put them back in the bag?

Am I a very selfish girl because I want my mother home with me and not in California finding her authentic self ??

Oh yes. I also have very bad thoughts and ~~evil intentions~~ toward one ARNOLD ARKVARD who makes fun of my hair. I ~~promise~~ to TRY to be a good girl and activate my gifts. Please teach me how to activate my gifts. Amen.

P.S. please don't lower the dreaded ax of fate upon me, please.

I dressed in my jeans and sneakers, glad it was Saturday. I had all day to try to work on my attitude. The first thing I did was four whole entire pages of math homework. And I worked on my poem like Miss Kreek wanted.

"You can't find *what?*" said Great Aunt Twill, while sitting in the chair pulling on her lumberjack boots.

"My Kidz Bible," I said. "I have to start studying it."

"Use mine," she said. "You'll know it on the shelf by all the papers stuck in it."

"Thank you, but I really want my own Bible. May I go down to the basement and look for it in our things?"

She gave a big harrumph. "If you make a mess down there, you're cleaning it up, hear me? I'm not your *maid*, you know. You kids think parents and adults are your *servants*. Do I look like a *servant?*"

She stood up, slung her red velvet cape over her skinny shoulders and stared at me hard. She looked like she was about to start a conversation. I didn't *want* her to start a conversation. I *wanted* to go down to the basement and find my Bible so I could obey Harold. I wanted to get started on doing good deeds to avoid the dreaded axe of fate.

"Bellflower, I know all about kids and their selfish little brains. You aren't the *only* kid to ever live in this house! " She said like she expected a reaction. "Did you hear me, Little Missy?"

Oh. OK. "Yes, Ma'am, I heard you. May I go now?" (Hey, wait a second. What was that?? I wasn't the *only* kid to live in this house?)

"Wha-what happened to them?" I gulped.

"Grew up of course!"

"You had kids of your own?

"A son," she said.

(I wondered where he slept.) "I didn't know you had a son, Great Aunt Twill." This was a *big* surprise.

"Well, I did and I do."

"I gave that boy everything he's got," and she gave the table a pounding with her bony hand. "I *made* him who he is today. I'm the one *responsible* for his success, and what *gratitude* do I get? Do I get any gratitude? No! Here it is almost Christmas time, and I bet he'll just *ignore* his poor mother…."

She looked so forlorn and unhappy. For an instant I felt sorry for her. Then she said something that snapped me back to reality. "My boy, Tellride, is gone and I'm all *alone* in this life," and she gave out a most pathetic moan.

(I ask you. Why is it adults think they're alone when *I'm* around? I could still hear my mother raving on and on about being all alone in life when there I was, sitting right next to her. Now here I am, right under Great Aunt Twill's nose and she considers herself all alone.)

"Hey," I said, without thinking. "Don't be so sad. Tellride might not be around, but tah-dah!—you've got *me*."

She looked at me with an expression on her face that I had never seen before. It looked something like a mix between a grin and a burp.

"*You*, Bellflower?"

"*Me*. You got *me* now." I felt stupid saying it, but like I said, at that moment I felt sorry for her.

She looked like she might topple over, but instead she sank into a chair. "You don't get it, do you?" she said in a hard, cold voice. The almost-smile was gone.

"I don't get what?" I said.

"You might be smart, but you just don't *get* it."

I fumbled with my hands, not knowing what else to do. Finally I came up with, "Why haven't I heard of Tellride?" (Come to think of it, how come I had never heard of Great Aunt Twill until I was dumped on her doorstep?)

She leaned forward on her chair and gave me one of her squinty-eye looks. "You don't even know who you are, do you?" she said.

My stomach went hollow. I felt dizzy. "Well, sure, I know who I am..." I stammered, "I see myself in the mirror every day and I say to myself, 'There I am, me,

Bellflower Munch...."' I paused for about three and a half seconds and added, "And Jesus loves me!"

Great Aunt Twill shut her eyes. "I'm tired," she said. "I'm plain tuckered out." Before I could say another word, she was asleep.

(But hey, wasn't she supposed to be going somewhere? Oh well.)

I tried to wake her up by blowing on her eyebrows like my mother always did to me, but she began snoring and I knew she was completely zonked. I wouldn't be getting any more information out of her for now.

What strange people adults are. I'd never figure them out. They are loaded with outrageous mysteries and secrets and who-knows-what-all. I would have to tell Skoot about this new development. Maybe he knew something about Tellride.

Meanwhile I had to get down to the basement and find my Bible so I wouldn't disappoint Jesus and Harold.

The basement was as dark as the attic, and twice as cold. It was the first time I had seen our things from the apartment since I came to Lake Clearbottom. It gave me a queasy feeling to see our curio cabinet on its side on the floor, and my mother's vanity without the mirror. Boxes were stacked against the wall next to our old sofa, which was covered with plastic garbage bags. I climbed on it and hugged a cushion.

Maybe it was my fault my mother left me. Maybe I was a terrible person like Great Aunt Twill's Tellride. But no, God forgives us when we ask, and Harold said God loved me.

I wondered what would make someone be mean to Great Aunt Twill. Maybe her son ate too many marshmallows and it made his brain go goopy.

I found my Bible in a box with our bamboo place mats, an empty peanut butter jar and a bunch of unopened bills from the telephone company. My mother was a good record keeper. She tossed her bills in a box every month. Sometimes she paid the bills in full, depending. She had a lot of responsibility, after all, and "oh how difficult it was for a woman alone with a child," like she always said, "in today's world."

I opened my Bible: *"Don't let your heart be troubled..."* Immediately the cold air in the basement became warmer. "OK," I said. "I won't let my heart be troubled. I won't."

I read more. *"Neither be afraid."* Right on. "I won't be afraid. I won't be afraid."

I came to the words, *"I will not leave you an orphan. I will come to you."*

(There was that word, orphan.)

God meant every word He ever said, didn't He? God would never say something to just blow in the breeze, right? He wouldn't fudge around for the heck of it, would He? He was *God.* I could trust every promise, right?

I read more of the Gospel of John. *"For God so loved the world that He gave His only beloved Son's life for us and whoever believes in Him has everlasting life."* We learned that verse in Sunday School in the King James version. I got a chocolate bar with almonds for memorizing it.

Every week we would get a candy bar for memorizing and reciting our Bible verses in front of the class. (Between the chocolate bars and the Oreo cookies I was set for the whole week.) I wanted to wow the class by memorizing the complete chapter of Ephesians 6 about fighting the devil with the whole armor of God—but we moved.

The basement door upstairs opened and Great Aunt Twill hollered down. "Bell, are you still down there?"

"Yes Ma'am."

"Have you frozen to death yet?"

"No, Ma'am."

"Well, get yourself upstairs this instant. I don't want to be gathering up any pieces of a frozen ten-year-old girl from my basement!"

"Eleven. I'm eleven years old."

The odd thing was, I didn't feel cold until she mentioned it. My breath made frost puffs in the air and my feet felt a little stiff, but I didn't feel cold.

"What on earth are you *doing* down there? I close my eyes for an instant and off you go to the basement without a coat! You better not have caught *pneumonia*! I'm *not* paying a fortune and sending you to a doctor and throwing away good money on medications for you!"

"Don't let your heart be troubled," I told her in the sweetest voice I could muster up. (I wanted to tell her about Harold the angel, but maybe it wasn't the right time.)

"What was that?" she shouted. "Are you being fresh with me, Little Missy? Listen here, don't you *dare* catch pneumonia!"

"Yes, Ma'am," I said, and started up the stairs.

"It's time for your *chores*, and you can start by making us a little lunch!"

Who, me? Make lunch? I raced past her to the kitchen before she changed her mind. Here was my chance to eat something besides marshmallows! *Thank you, Lord.*

I was somewhat experienced in the cooking department because my mother worked late at the hair salon most nights and she liked to have her supper waiting when she got home. (Her lo-fat microwave dinners mostly.) I never felt I was destined for anything other than mediocrity at the stove, but I felt different now. (*Mediocrity*: really boring.)

What did Aunt Twill keep in her cupboards anyhow?

I couldn't help but sing as I twirled around in the kitchen rummaging through Great Aunt Twill's sacred cupboards and drawers, all of which had been off limits to me until now. I found some carrots and celery in the back of the crisper in the refrigerator, and a fat tomato.

Hidden behind a jar of molasses was a piece of chicken wrapped in waxed paper with half an onion.

I found flour in the cupboard and a can of shortening. Singing in a soft voice so Great Aunt Twill wouldn't get suspicious, I lit the oven and began chopping vegetables.

Finally, I called Great Aunt Twill and Lady Mae to the table for lunch.

"What's *this*?!" they gasped when they saw the table set with three steaming bowls of peanut butter-chicken soup, a fresh chopped salad bowl, and a plate of baking powder biscuits hot from the oven.

"*You* made this meal? *You*?"

Let it be said, they were shocked.

They took their seats and Great Aunt Twill recited her usual blessing that went something like, "God is great, God is good, and for this which we are about to partake, bless this food to our bodies, thanks a lot, Amen."

They began gobbling. They gobbled up the soup and the hot biscuits first. (Lady Mae ate six biscuits and two bowls of soup.) Then the salad.

"How in Heaven's name," chomp chomp, "did you accomplish this? Where did you," slurp slurp, "learn to cook, you useless child?" Great Aunt Twill asked when she finished the last drop of soup and crumb of biscuit.

(In Heaven's name! Yes, that was it! Heaven!) "I got a little creative is all," I said.

"Do tell," said Lady Mae. "What else can you do?"

"Nothing, probably," I said.

She held her spoon in the air. "Nothing? But this meal is *delicious*. She leaned back in her chair and belched a few times to make her point.

It was then when I figured out what the mysterious black goop was Lady Mae's mouth was always full of. She reached in her pocket and pulled out a can of tobacco and set it on the table. Chewing tobacco.

"What you staring at, girl? Haven't you ever seen chaw before?"

"No, Ma'am."

Just then the phone rang. I jumped up to answer it because I knew by the time either of them got out of their chairs and across the room to the telephone, the person calling would have given up.

It was Skoot. He wanted to know if I'd help him write another poem.

"Skoot," I whispered, "Do you know anything about my Great Aunt Twill's son, Tellride?"

"Don't *whisper*," yelled Great Aunt Twill. "It's *rude*!" She was helping herself to another biscuit.

I made up something quick in a loud voice: "Um. Skoot, do you WANT TO DO OUR HOMEWORK TOGETHER?"

He said OK, but at his house.

"Great Aunt Twill, may I go over to Skoot's house and do homework?"

"No."

I held the receiver in the palm of my hand and asked in a sweet voice, "Great Aunt Twill, will you listen to my poem then? Will you let me practice reading my poem with *stanzas* to you?"

"Just how many stanzas are you planning? ...Oh! That could go on for *hours*...all right, you can go over to Skoot's," she said. "But only after you finish your chores."

"How long will that take?" Skoot wanted to know.

"How long will that take?" I asked Great Aunt Twill.

She said how was she to know, was she a time clock, and please to stop bothering her whilst partaking of a biscuit. Then she gave a big harrumph.

"So you're a poet now, too, Bellflower?" asked Lady Mae.

"Not exactly, Ma'am," I said. "My teachers say I have some potential, probably. And I'm just trying to activate a gift." I gave her a big smile, a real one, not one of my not-nice pretend smiles.

Great Aunt Twill snorted in her biscuit. "I knew it. The girl's not right in the head."

I did my chores as fast as I could because I could hardly wait to see Skoot to ask him about Tellride.

Personal Private KEEP OUT this means YOU Journal

**Hot From the Oven Baking Powder Biscuits**

⅓ cup shortening
1-¾ cups ALL Purpose Flour
2-½ teaspoons baking powder
1 cup milk
¾ teaspoon salt

Heat oven to 450°
Mix shortening into the flour, baking powder and salt with two knives, or a fork, or a thing called a pastry blender until the dough gets crumbly. Start stirring in the milk until the dough leaves the side of the bowl and rounds up into a ball. Drop the dough by spoonfuls onto a greased cookie sheet. Bake until golden brown, about 10 to 12 minutes.

When they're hot, break open and spread
with mustard & mayonnaise spread.
Mustard & Mayonnaise Spread:
1 teaspoon mustard
2 Tablespoons (OR more) mayonnaise (or Miracle Whip)
½ teaspoon sugar
Mix all together and spread on biscuits
like butter.

You can create all sorts of FUN BISCUITS
with this recipe just by adding whatever you
like to the dough like apples or
peaches or whatever! And you can
spread anything on top. Like peanut butter.
--Even a marshmallow or two!!
(ha ha)

# 10

## The Bittle Surprise

I cleaned the kitchen. I scrubbed the floor. I polished the windows. I finished every one of the chores on my list. Outside a friendly little spattering of snow brushed across the ground. Without snow everything looked brown and dead and sad. Great Aunt Twill waited for me at the front door in her cape and bonnet and big boots.

"I'll drive you to the Bittle's house," she said. "I don't want you coming down with the grip being out there in the cold. No telling *what* might happen to you. You could catch *pneumonia*. You could get buried alive in a snow drift!"

Snow drift? "Thanks," I said, trying to imagine what it would be like being buried alive in about six flakes. We climbed into her big old Buick and she started wrestling with the engine. After four and a half tries, she got it revved up.

"You're taking a big load off Lady Mae," she told me. "Lady Mae has always done the cleaning, but she can't move around quite as easy as she used to."

"How come? Is it because she's so fat?" which I thought was an innocent enough question, being Lady Mae didn't seem to do much except eat and chew tobacco.

Great Aunt Twill slammed on the brake which made me jerk forward and almost clunk my head on the dashboard. Before I had a chance to say "ouch," she started in. Boy was she angry.

"You don't know what that woman's been through!" she yelled. "Sometimes there are folks who the world just doesn't understand."

Like me, for instance, is what I wanted to say.

Great Aunt Twill shook her hand in my face and went on. "Ain't nothing wrong with Lady Mae! Don't you be saying anything bad about Lady Mae. I promised myself I'd help and take care of the poor dear the best I could after the sorrow she's suffered. Just because there are things you don't know don't give you the right to be uppity!"

"She hates me," I said.

"So? I don't like you much either."

When we arrived at the Bittle's house Great Aunt Twill pulled in the driveway at such a speed we almost went right through the kitchen.

Skoot was glad to see me and his mother invited Great Aunt Twill in for a cup of tea. She declined, huffing no, no, absolutely not. She had to get home to feed the cats.

"I didn't know you had cats," said Skoot.

"We don't," I said.

Great Aunt Twill left and Skoot's mother told me to hang up my jacket in the hall and take off my boots so they wouldn't get her floor muddy. "My, that's some car that woman's got," she said rather astonished. "You know, I've known your aunt a long time and she always gives me the cold shoulder. All because of me communicating with—oh never mind."

Communicating with whom? There it was again. Adults harboring secrets. Lake Clearbottom was full of secrets.

Skoot's mother stood gawking at me for a long time. "My, my, my. Who did you inherit all that hair from?"

I was immediately self-conscious. My hair was one big snarled fur wad. I forgot to comb and press it down. Skoot's mother blinked, shook her head. "And you're so thin!"

Skoot's mother put me in mind of the mothers you see in the pictures of Sunday School take-home papers and old TV programs. Those mothers were always pretty, with rosy cheeks, respectable clothes, and nice teeth. They never had much to do and they were always real nice. I never believed they were *real* moms.

Skoot's mother liked to sew. You might say she had a real *thing* for sewing. She had stitched almost everything in the house! Curtains, pillows, wall hangings, appliance covers, rugs, blankets, towels (even the toilet seat cover—embroidered, I discovered).

All the furniture was covered with something stitched by her. "Yes, dear, I enjoy sewing. I even knit all the socks in this family," she said, beaming with pride.

"In fact, I knit sweaters, afghans—you name it. …Tell me, does your mother knit?"

"No, but once in a while she does the laundry," I said.

Skoot and I sat on the floor in the Bittle family room to do our homework. The floor was covered with little rugs his mother had braided. Skoot's three-ring notebook was covered in felt with a cowboy on a horse appliquéd on the cover.

"Maybe she'll sew one for you if you ask her."

"Naw. That's OK."

"Let's get this over with. My stink-wad sister will be home soon."

"You shouldn't call your sister a stink-wad," I said, surprising myself.

"Why not? You should hear what she calls me."

For some reason I didn't like hearing that. Ordinarily it wouldn't have fazed me because I knew lots of kids who despised their brothers and sisters. One boy in my fifth grade class last year lit a firecracker under his sister's chair and she had to go to the hospital. My mother said that was the way it was in this world. You just never could tell when some goofus might fire explosives under your hinder.

"Listen, Skoot, do me a favor, and don't say bad things about anyone, OK?"

"Sure, yeah, but what's with you? You seem different." he said.

"I've been talking to an angel is all," I said.

He laughed so hard he fell over onto his mother's hand-crocheted ottoman.

"Say, where's your dog, Rabbit?" I said, changing the subject.

"She's been banished to the backyard," Skoot said. "She chewed one too many dust ruffles." We finished our math assignment and I wrote a poem with four actual stanzas.

"Skoot, did you know my Great Aunt Twill has a son?" I said finally.

"No," said Skoot.

"Well sure enough, she has a son!" yelled Skoot's mother, who had been listening from the next room where she sat quilting. "That would be Tellride!"

I found out Tellride was pals with someone named Robert, who happened to be Lady Mae's only son.

"Lady Mae has a son, *too*?" I shook my head to clear the cobwebs. How come everything was so *secret* around that house?

"Sure, and they graduated from Lake Clearbottom High, like me and like Mr. Bittle; and they played on the football team and were popular with the girls—Robert especially, that would be Lady Mae's boy." (So where were they now?) "But then Tellride wasn't that bad looking either, he being more the strong, silent type."

"Where are they now?" I bellowed out.

"Tellride and Robert? Robert's gone," she said, her mouth all pinched up.

"Gone?"

"Yes, a crying shame it is, too. Lady Mae's never been the same. And Tellride, well, he just sort of went off on his own somewhere. Last I heard he was going to architecture school, if there is such a thing. Oh, I shouldn't be talking about these matters. I shouldn't say anymore."

"Where is Tellride now?" I prodded.

"Why don't you ask your aunt about Tellride's whereabouts?"

"I don't think my aunt and Tellride are on speaking terms."

"Yes, well, the accident and all…"

"The accident?"

Just then Skoot's 16-year-old sister, Tamara, burst through the door. "I'm home! I'm home! Have you all been waiting for me? Everyone can rejoice! I'm home!"

I liked her right off.

"Oh great," said Skoot who almost said something mean, but then remembered his promise to me. "Ignore her, Bell. Come on, I'll walk you home."

"Hey, who's your girlfriend, little man?" Tamara squealed.

Before Skoot could speak, I introduced myself.

"Bellflower? What kind of a name is Bellflower?" she said with a snort of a laugh.

"My kind of name, probably," I said. She sized me up with the superior smirk older kids give you, and then she said, "So you're the one using my skates which my dear darling brother took without *asking*."

"Hey, I'm sorry," I said, trying to avoid a battle. "I'm glad you're here now so I can thank you in person. Thanks!"

"Yeah, well, they don't fit me anyhoo." She stood back sizing me up. She was looking at my hair. "Hmm, how did you get that thingy on top? That is like so awesome!"

(I hadn't combed my hair since yesterday.)

"My hair," I said pulling my shoulders back, "is a gift from God."

"Ooo-ee," she squealed. "A gift from God! I like that, ooo-ee," and she bounced off to her room cackling.

We could hear her on the telephone with her girlfriend talking about boys. "So anyhow, like this is like so totally awesome," she was saying. "Get this. I go 'Hello' and he goes 'Hello yourself,' so I go 'What's new,' and he goes 'New York, New Jersey, New Hampshire'.... And I go 'Ha Ha'! And he goes, 'Whatever.' I'm so totally sure he like, *likes* me!"

"She's hopeless," said Skoot.

Great Aunt Twill was in no mood for questions when I got home. She was in her nightgown and bathrobe ready to go to bed, and it was only six o'clock. A bowl of marshmallows and a glass of bugleaid sat on the table for my supper.

"Tomorrow's Sunday and we're going to the early service, if you can drag yourself out of the sack," she told me. "As for me, I'm very, very tired. I need my sleep. Don't forget to turn out the lights," and she disappeared into her room.

I sighed, pleased to have the opportunity to sit in the parlor where it was warm, and read my Bible. I climbed onto the sofa and opened to the Book of Ephesians.

*...because of what Christ has done we have become gifts to God that he delights in* (Ephesians 1:11).

That means God delights in us. Can it be? Well, the Bible wouldn't lie, and that's what it says.

*Because of his kindness you have been saved through trusting Christ. And even trusting is not of yourselves; it too is a gift from God. Salvation is not a reward for the good we have done, so none of us can take any credit for it. It is God himself who has made us what we are and given us new lives from Christ Jesus; and long ages ago he planned that we should spend these lives in helping others* (Ephesians 2:8-10).

I know I must have read these words when we did our Ephesians worksheets in my old Sunday School, but it felt like I never heard them before. How come the words seemed brand new to me now? I have a new life in my Messiah, Jesus. This is good! He *loves* me! I believed God was kind and nice because that's what everybody said, but I never really *felt* it. I never really *felt* God's Word before.

### Revised Poem by Bellflower Munch

(*in stanzas*)

In the long months of winter comes
a promise; one that could melt ice

in an instant with the taste of surprise,
a surprise more perfect and beautiful
than anything you can name, and that surprise

is hearing from Heaven. Who would guess
a thing like that is possible in this cold
world when we live so far from Heaven's
shores? Who would guess God would speak
to me, a girl with bad hair and an attitude,

and a pimple coming up on her chin? Well,
I'm here to say it did happen. Now the ice
melts, the pouting mouth of winter turns
glad, and so do I because all the world
sings when Harold sings "hark," which means

listen. If God will help me listen, I will
do that every single day from now on
and I am glad to do what He tells me
because that is the only way to be happy,
and I miss my mother. The end.

# 11

## An Incredible Journey Consisting of Supernatural Events

I got a sudden dreaded thought: Did my new life mean I'd be forced to live with Great Aunt Twill until I was old and decrepit? Would my mother never come for me?

I got to thinking. Well, OK, I belong to Jesus. I suppose that means I should try to make the best of it here in rotten old Lake Clearbottom. If I can't change *things*, I can change *me*. Probably.

After all, I told myself, there were a million mysteries yet to solve.

It was late when I turned out the lights and climbed up the ladder to the attic. I thought about what it says in Ephesians, about me being made in Christ's image. About how I was alive with Him and made to sit together in heavenly places with Him. It just seemed too incredible. Me? Sit with in heavenly places with Jesus?

If the Bible was written for us to understand and know God for ourselves, then it was an extremely *personal* book, right? The Bible was God's Holy Word for everyone, sure, I knew that, but it was also written for each of us *personally*, right? That meant I could read His words as a personal message to me, right? This was all so new to me.

How come it took me this long to get interested in the Word of God?

I crept on my knees to my mattress and made a nose dive under the covers. I felt happy enough to sing. I always sang "Ninety-nine Bottles of Beer on the Wall" to my mother when she couldn't sleep at night, but that just wouldn't do for now. I started to hum "Jesus Loves Me" when I got a strange feeling that I wasn't alone.

"Harold, is that you?"

"Yes," said Harold, "It is I."

Oh joy. HaroldHaroldHarold.

"The Lord sent me with another message for you," he said in his beautiful Harold voice.

I sat up and rubbed my eyes. Harold had returned! I wanted to jump up and down but I'd give myself a concussion crashing into the rafters.

"I've been reading my Bible, you know, just like you told me to do," I said.

"I only bring the message. It is the Lord who gave you the message to read your Bible," said Harold.

"Oh yes. OK, you bring the message from Him. You're a real honest-to-God angel. I'm afraid I don't know much about angels."

"The Bible speaks of angels over 300 times," said Harold.

I held still. If I nodded my head it might look like I already knew that.

"Angels are created spirits," he continued, "and if the Lord gives us the order, we are permitted to make ourselves known to humans. In other words, even though we are invisible to your human world, we can suddenly become visible if God wills it."

(And he came to *me*.)

Harold stood in his beautiful light and said, "We angels are oracles of God. We think, feel, and have emotions; and we often bring divine messages from God to humans. Read the Book of Hebrews in your Bible, Bellflower. Read Hebrews chapter 1, verse 14. Go ahead."

"OK." I fumbled for my Bible and read out loud:

*"Are they* [angels] *not all ministering spirits?"*

"But don't confuse us with the Holy Spirit," said Harold. Angels don't live *inside* human beings, that's the job of the Holy Spirit."

"Does the Holy Spirit live in me?" I asked with a gulp.

"Yes, Bellflower. When you gave your life to the Lord Jesus, the Holy Spirit took up residence within you. Can you understand that?"

"Yes, I think so," I said with another gulp. "He moved in."

"That's right."

I was eager to tell him about the good things that had happened since his first visit. "Guess what," I said, "I prepared the best meal I ever tried to cook all by myself. I made biscuits and everything."

"I know. I was there with you."

*"You were with me?"*

"Bellflower, even though you can't see me, I am always watching over you. I am your guardian angel."

(Time out for a great big whoop, hands-in-the-air YESS!)

"Is Jesus with me, too?"

"Of course! He will never leave you or forsake you. And Holy Spirit is alive *in* you. You see, the Holy Spirit can be everywhere at the same time. We angels can only be in one place at a time."

It boggled my brain. I was beginning to see that the spiritual world was so much greater than I ever imagined. Whatever makes us think the visible world is all there is?

Harold sat down beside me. "Bellflower, God is giving you many gifts and it's up to you to use them well."

"Gifts? As in Christmas gifts? Does He wrap them and everything?"

"*Spiritual* gifts, dear. The kind that last. The gifts you receive wrapped in paper won't last forever. When our heavenly Father gives gifts, they are forever."

(Yes, but I could use some new mittens, I thought. And some decent shoes.)

Harold shot me the sweetest smile you ever saw. "Bellflower," he said, "I live in the presence of God, and I've come with a message for you."

"A message? For me?"

"Yes. I've come to help you be ready for things to come."

I felt a shiver. "You mean *bad* things?"

"Trust in the Lord with all your heart. This is the key to overcoming all trials," he said lifting his hands out to me.

I reached for Harold's hands and was shocked to discover they were made of *light!* Not possible! When I looked closer, his whole body became surrounded with an aura of light so brilliant it burned my eyes.

"The Lord God almighty wants to show you things in the heavenly realm. He wants to show you great things in heavenly places."

I gasped. "Does that mean I'm going to die?"

"You don't have to die to visit heavenly places, but you must belong to Jesus and you must have His Spirit living in you. Holy Spirit will guide us on the journey we're about to take together."

"I'm not sure I understand," I said, stammering and a little frightened.

"Oh Bellflower, most humans don't understand. They just don't realize that God has many more blessings for them than they take. Most humans settle for little dabs of what God has to give. They don't understand what it is to live in His power and His blessings. They don't understand *Him*."

(I felt like apologizing for the whole world, which would be stupid, right?)

Harold gave me a patient smile. "There is much for you to learn, dear one. Change begins with one's self first."

(I would write that down later. So much to learn!) I took a breath and ventured, "May I ask you a question? It's something I've wondered about, and you're the perfect one to ask."

"Go right ahead."

"My question is about when Jesus was born and the host of angels showed up in the sky over Bethlehem…"

"I remember it like yesterday!" Harold exclaimed. "What a glorious day! We continue to celebrate to this day! We can't stop marveling at the passionate heart of God."

"We?"

"Yes. All of the billions of us who make up God's angelic hosts."

(Billions. He said billions.)

"You can be sure God's angelic hosts are everywhere and we are great in number. Now I have a question for you."

"A question for me?"

"Yes. Are you ready to take a journey with me?"

"You're serious? A *journey*?"

"Yes. A journey."

"Wait. I'll change clothes."

"No need. Just take my hand."

Harold reached out his hand to me and I took it. I was actually holding the hand of an angel! Me, Bellflower Much, holding the hand of an angel!

Suddenly we were lifted up into the air. Up above the floor, above the rafters, above the roof, above the house...up, up...right into the night sky. We went soaring into the sky as smooth and easy as kites in the wind. I didn't feel at all cold. I didn't even feel silly wearing pajamas. It felt wonderful to be soaring in the sky with Harold.

We flew higher and higher. I couldn't see Lake Clearbottom below us anymore. I couldn't see anything below us.

"Back to my question," I called out, "Did the angels sing in the sky when Jesus was born or did they just shout out the news?"

"Ah! You are a smart girl! Yes, what a smart question. Darling girl. Angels sing *all* the time. Our songs are filled with praises and glory to God. We love to sing and praise God, just love it."

"I would love to learn some new songs, Harold. Will you teach me some songs?"

"Ask Holy Spirit to sing in your heart. What fills your heart will come out of your mouth. Holy Spirit will help you."

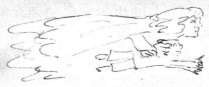

I started humming, and then I put words to the humming. I sang, *Glory to God in the highest* because the Bible says those are the words the angels sing. Harold joined right in. I sang other words, too. Words like *praise the Lord* and *Hallelujah*, and *thank you, Jesus*. We sang and sang, and I wanted to never stop.

I began to understand that when we worship God in church, or wherever, the angels sing with us! It doesn't matter what our voices sound like. What matters is what's in our hearts.

The night was changing colors now, becoming lighter, brighter.

"Look ahead of you, Bellflower, what do you see?"

I looked ahead of me and saw what appeared to be a city in the sky. It was bright and shiny.

"I think I see a city," I said. "But it doesn't look like any city on earth. It doesn't even look like Minneapolis. The buildings are like castles!"

I saw a blaze of light above the city and a blinding orb of the brightest gold. Everything in the city sparkled like diamonds must sparkle probably.

"Where are we, Harold?"

"Look and you will understand."

We flew closer to the city and I could see glittery paved streets and lustrous walls of buildings. We flew closer to the orb of gold hovering over the city. Closer and closer we came to the brightness of the gold. My eyes stung with the burning presence of the gold, but we continued to move closer. I clung to Harold, breathless and in a state of total wonder.

The gold wasn't stationery. I saw it moving. Then to my shock I saw that it was an actual being. Was I dreaming? I was not dreaming. Angels all around me were singing. I was surrounded by singing angels.

The Being was completely clothed in gold and glimmering so bright that I knew my eyes would drop out of their sockets if I tried to look directly at Him. I saw huge objects flying around Him. The objects were gold and they looked like rockets, or like huge missiles—these torrents of gold projectiles cascaded all around the Being. As I squinted in the blinding light, I suddenly realized that the Being before me was none other than the Lord Jesus Himself.

Could it be? Could it be?

"Yes, dear one," Harold breathed in my ear. "It is the Lord." With that he burst into a song of praise with all the angels, and I joined in too. *"Oh Lord Jesus, you are so great! You are so beautiful! You are so glorious!"*

I couldn't help myself. One glimpse of the King of kings and I just couldn't help myself. *Wonderful! Magnificent! Incredible! Outrageous!*

Then I saw the most amazing thing. All of those flying gold objects hurling around the Lord were multiplying by the second. Some of the objects looked dangerous, like they might break something or explode. Some looked refined and polished, others looked ordinary and plain.

Some of the gold pieces were beautiful and cared for. Some were frayed, falling apart. The Lord tenderly gathered every single throbbing clump in His arms, one at a time. As far as my eye could see, these chunks of gold rushed at Him like artillery. The Lord Jesus caught each one, held each one, and hugged them to His chest.

"These are the prayers of His children," Harold whispered in my ear. "The Lord cares for *every* prayer."

I was speechless.

"The Lord answers every prayer, dear one. Sometimes the answer is no. Sometimes the answer is wait. But always His answers emanate from perfect love." (*Emanate:* come out from.)

Would I ever get my voice back?

The Lord *hugs* our prayers!

Harold put his beautiful face near my ear. "Remember, dear one, God answers every single prayer you pray. That's why it's very important to be careful with His name. People speak the name of God as if it were just another word. They don't realize what they're doing— they are beckoning God!"

That was scary. I knew lots of people who said God's name all the time, and they sure weren't praying. What would happen to them?

At that instant, the Lord turned and looked at me. His was face so full of love and goodness I could have fizzled to ashes right there. He smiled at me and I wanted to climb into that smile and never leave. I wanted to rush into the arms that held all those prayers. I was completely covered in the smile of God.

I realized I was crying. I couldn't help myself. It was all so incredible.

"Don't forget," whispered Harold, "God hears and answers His children's prayers. *Remember*."

# 12

## The All-New Bellflower

The next day happened to be Sunday and I decided to perform an act of charity and help Lady Mae overcome the nasty tobacco habit. Finding those black wads of chewed tobacco around the house wasn't exactly the most pleasant of experiences. I made a plan. Before church on Sunday I would gather up her little cans of tobacco and stuff them in my jacket pockets. Then I'd find a garbage can somewhere and toss them. I just knew she'd be glad I did!

Boy, was I wrong. I accomplished everything as planned and was about to climb into Great Aunt Twill's car for church when there came a roar from within the house like Leo the Lion had stepped in a nest of hornets. The door flew open and out trounced Lady Mae. She tore after me, her chubby legs racing like little propellers.

"Stop! Thief! Thief!"

"What on earth...?" Great Aunt Twill grunted. "Where's the thief?"

"*She's* the thief! *Bellflower*! She's got my chaw!"

I ducked into the car, but Lady Mae yanked open the door and dragged me out by my foot. "Hand'er over!"

"Ow," I squeaked. There was no use denying I had what she wanted in my jacket pockets.

"Think you can steal from me, eh?"

She emptied my pockets and set me back in the car. With my foot still in the door, she slammed it shut. I was sure my little toe was chopped off, but when I got to church, there it was, still safe in my sock, but red and sore enough to make my ears burn.

"You ought not mess with Lady Mae's chaw," Great Aunt Twill scolded me. "She'll give up the habit when she has a mind to. And put your sock back on. You're in *church*, girl."

Pastor Schlinmbim read to us from the 91st Psalm. "That's it! That's it!" I cried out. "He will give His angels charge over us…Don't you see, Great Aunt Twill, *everyone*? That's *true*! God gave His angels to watch over us!"

Great Aunt Twill gave me a huge poke in the stomach. "Hush, girl!"

"But God really *has* given us angels! I *know*!"

She covered her nose with her shawl. She wasn't wearing her combat boots today, being Sunday. Instead she wore her flamenco dancing shoes—and she gave my foot a kick with her heel.

"But God has given us angels...OUCH!...Harold is one of them!" (She got me on my good foot.)

After church, Skoot caught up with me in the narthex where everybody shakes everybody's hand and says, "How lovely to see you" and "How have you been" and "How's the plumbing holding up in this weather."

Skoot was desperate to go to Marvelous Marvels for ice cream. Great Aunt Twill said, "In *this* weather? Are you crazy in the head? It's freezing out. Who eats ice cream in this weather? Besides, I don't want any kin of mine going to *that* place."

Another mystery. "But why? What's wrong with ice cream?" I said.

"Nothing is wrong with ice cream. Ice cream is perfectly fine if eaten with appreciation. It's just that place! It's...it's...oh, all right, so go ahead. Go eat ice cream and freeze your tonsils! But don't come running to me with frozen tonsils begging to be nursed! I'll just say I *told* you so!"

"Thanks," I said in my new sweet, cheery voice. I knew there was something else on Skoot's mind besides ice cream. He only got this excited when there was trouble close by. He was in the mood for a Storm Sundae, he said, (wink, wink) which is chocolate ice cream, pineapple jam, and M&M's. What on earth was he up to? He was on to something.

I was anxious to tell Skoot about Harold, my angel, and my trip up to Heaven where I saw the Lord Jesus with all those prayers whizzing around Him.

"OK, what's the real reason we're going to Marvelous Marvels?" I asked, winking back at him.

"I think there's something mighty bizarre going on over there," he said in a voice loaded with mystery.

"*Everything* is bizarre in this town," I said, (except for Harold, of course) but I knew Skoot had something up his sleeve, and that something was not ice cream.

He took in a breath like an important specialist in crime and said, "I can see their windows from my room and there are lights on at all hours of the night. Not only that, each night there's the same *truck* parked in front. Now I ask you, who hangs around ice cream all night in the dead of winter? Nobody, that's who. I think Miss Marvelous is doing more than scooping ice cream is what I think."

"I think I'm getting hungry for chocolate ice cream, pineapple jam, and M&M's, is what I think," I said, pulling up my jacket hood and snapping it under my chin. An adventure sounded like fun, especially if it had something to do with ice cream. And I'd tell him about Harold and what I saw in the heavenly place.

Miss Marvelous greeted us with smiles and chuckles and grins, like we were her best customers in weeks, months, years.

"Hey, howzit going, kids? Some hot chocolate for ya?"

"We'd like two Storm Sundaes, please, Missus Marvelous."

"Missus? I'm not a Missus. Call me Miz Marvelous, thank you very much."

"*Miz* Marvelous? Sorry. OK. We'd like two Storm Sundaes, Miz Marvelous." Skoot sounded very official.

Miz Marvelous began scooping our ice cream and Skoot gave me a big nudge. "Ask to use the rest room," he said.

"Why? I don't have to go."

"Just do it."

"No. You."

"Come on, Bell. Girls always have to use the restroom. You ask her. Then look around and see if you see anything suspicious."

The restroom was at the end of a dark, crowded storage area. I felt around the wall for a light switch and flicked it on. Nothing but supply boxes of detergent, napkins, ice cream cones, frozen yogurt mix, and cans of syrup—strawberry, cherry, chocolate, peach. A basket of green bananas perched on top of a gallon jug of cocoa mix.

I crawled around the boxes looking for a clue of some sort. But a clue of what? Just then I saw a door hidden behind the boxes. A *hidden door*. Oh, Skoot was going to love this. I felt around for a doorknob. I squeezed between the boxes, gave the door a push, but it was locked. I got down on my knees and tried to peer underneath the door. By pressing my face on the floor, I could see stairs leading down to a basement. But when I squeezed in closer, I got a real shock. At the bottom of

the stairs I could see a little desk and something on the desk. In the dim light, I recognized it immediately because I saw one like it every day—our *math book*! With my excellent eyesight I thought it was actually open to tomorrow's homework on decimals (which I still hadn't finished).

Then I heard something move and I jerked back as fast as I could. My heart was beating so hard I was sure it could be heard all the way in Pennsylvania or Oklahoma probably.

Someone was locked up in the dungeon down there! And why were they studying *decimals*!?

The sundaes were on the counter when I joined Skoot.

"Four dollars," said Miz Marvelous.

"I'm paying," said Skoot. "I know your aunt probably doesn't give you much allowance, Bell."

I was still shaking from what I'd just seen. I gave a shrug. "My mother used to give me an allowance, but she always took it back when she ran out of hair spray or color rinse."

"You really should talk to your *aunt* about giving you an allowance," said Skoot.

"That's a laugh and a half," I said.

Miz Marvelous stayed close to us leaning on the counter. "What grade you kids in?" she said.

"Sixth," Skoot said.

"Yes, sixth," I said.

I watched her face. No change of expression. "That so? You kids go to Clearbottom Middle School or some swanky private school?"

Swanky private school? Was she kidding? Did she think we looked like rich, private school kids? Heck, I was wearing my third grade mittens.

The last thing in the world I wanted to do now was eat ice cream. Miz Marvelous watched me carefully as though she was taking notes in her head.

"You're new here, aren't you, girl?"

It occurred to me by the way she was staring at me that Miz Marvelous was a kidnapper probably! Whoever she had locked in the dungeon was a kidnapped kid she was holding for ransom!

"What's yer name, girl?" she said.

I looked at her large round face with big yellow curls covering her cheeks. Two or three curls fell down her forehead over her eyes.

"My name is Bellflower," I told her snapping an M&M in half with my front teeth.

"Bellflower? What kind of a moniker is that?"

"My father named me," I started to say, which is the lie I usually made up when people made fun of my name. I would tell them how my father adored flowers and how he adored me, etc., etc., but now I couldn't make myself tell a lie. I had never met my father in my entire life and I didn't feel like telling any more lies. Besides, nobody ever heard of a flower called Bellflower.

"Well, that's my name, Bellflower," I said.

"Ain't no flower called Bellflower," she said.

(Well, *duh!*) "Sorry," I said. "Guess I'm stuck with that slight botanical error."

I was itching to tell Skoot about the hidden door in the back. Maybe *this* was what Harold was warning me about. A big shiver ran through my entire body.

"May I have a glass of water please?" I said in a jittery voice.

"Water? You don't want water," said Miz Marvelous with a sly smile, "Water is so *ordinary*. How's about some of my yummy-for-the-tummy hot chocolate?"

"Sure!" said Skoot. "Make it two."

Miz Marvelous gave him a slippery grin and left us to pour hot chocolate from the urn at the end of the counter.

"Skoot," I whispered, "don't drink it. It could be drugged. Or *poisoned*."

"What? *What?*" he choked. "Did you discover something back there? Tell me. Tell me."

"Go in the back and check for yourself!"

"Excuse me, Ma'am," said Skoot, "but could I use the restroom?"

She didn't even look up. "Don't you kids have biffies at home?"

I jumped off the counter stool. "I'll show him where it is," I said, and led him behind the boxes and the canned syrups to the hidden door.

"It's locked, but you can see under it if you get down low enough," I whispered as quiet as I could. "Hurry up!"

He knelt down to look, and knocked over a box of frozen yogurt mix.

"Ohmygosh!" he squawked. "I can see a desk and books and…."

I heard Miz Marvelous' feet sliding across the floor toward the storage room.

"Quick!" I gasped, and pulled him away from the door. We were both on our hands and knees when Miz Marvelous saw us.

"What's going on, you two?" she squawked. "What are you up to? Trying to *steal* something, are you?"

"No, oh my, no," I said, trying to sound casual. "We just never saw so much chocolate syrup. In fact, I never knew chocolate syrup came in such big cans. My mother always bought chocolate syrup in those little tiny jars. You know? Tiny jars?"

Miz Marvelous glared at Skoot. "Hurry up and do your business, boy. Your drink will get cold. Put that frozen yogurt mix back where it belongs."

I returned to the counter and sat before a steaming cup of hot chocolate. To my dismay, a handful of miniature marshmallow floated on top. *Marshmallows.*

"Where you from, girl?" said Miz Marvelous.

"I'm from, from, um, from St. Paul," I said, and took in two spoonfuls of pineapple and chocolate ice cream, avoiding the hot chocolate.

"They teach you to steal in St. Paul?"

"No, Ma'am. I don't steal, Ma'am. Honest I don't. Neither does Skoot. Honest!"

"OK, OK, I believe you. So if you're from St Paul, what are you doing here in Lake Clearbottom?"

"I'm staying with my Great Aunt Twill. For a while. A very little while, probably."

"Twill? Over on Lilypad Avenue? I know her, of course." Then her eyes lit up like she came to a realization. "*Sure* I know Twill…Everybody knows her…and her poor sister, Lady Mae. Ever since the accident she's never has been the same."

"Accident? What accident?"

"You don't know? Well, there was an accident. That's all I'm saying."

Skoot returned to the counter looking pale. His hand shook when he tried to pick up his cup of hot chocolate.

Miz Marvelous watched him with a wary eye. "…'Course there's been a lot of boys turned up missing from these parts…"

I dropped my spoon. "Boys *missing*?"

"What with the war and what-not," she shrugged. "'Course you kids is too young…"

I gave Skoot a poke with my left foot. He winced like I had hurt him.

"And then there's sickness and disease," said Miz Marvelous dismally. "…Lots of pain in this here world."

I got a flash picture of Miz, not Missus, Marvelous poisoning children.

(Harold, where are you, Harold?)

"I have to get home," I said.

"You hardly touched your Storm," said Miz Marvelous. "Lookie here, you're much too skinny for a girl your age. You oughter eat one of my sundaes every day. I'll help you put some meat on them bones. And what about your hot chocolate?"

"I'm allergic to marshmallows," I said, jumping off the stool.

"Wait for me," said Skoot, taking his last and second-to-the-last big mouthfuls of ice cream. He was dripping pineapple jam as he counted out two dollars in quarters for the hot chocolates.

"They're on the house," said Miz Marvelous. "Put your quarters away."

Skoot took a swig of his hot chocolate. "Wow. Thanks," he said while scooping up his money.

"You kids come back now, hear? And don't even think about stealing something from me."

"Sure, oh sure, no, I mean, we would never..." I stammered.

"Right!" said Skoot.

Once outside we ran for two straight blocks without stopping. We were out of breath and my feet felt frozen solid. It must have been my boots. They weren't lined and I had holes in my socks.

"Who do you suppose she's got locked in her basement?" Skoot huffed, trying to catch his breath.

"*Dungeon*, you mean."

"You notice how she made a big thing about not calling her Missus? Wasn't that suspicious? Huh? Wasn't it? Suppose she's got a *husband* locked up in the basement?"

Now he was really freaking me out.

"Bell, we've got to try to help whoever is locked up down there escape. There must be a way to sneak inside. Maybe there's a window, a back door, something."

"Breaking and entering! That's three to five years, Skoot. Forget it. And suppose Miz Marvelous catches us? What if she locks us up, too?"

I kicked at the snow with my boot. "Skoot. Forget it."

I started to tell him about Harold and my trip to Heaven, but he jumped in with, "Bell, we *both* saw our math book sitting there big as life! *Somebody* down there is keeping up with our lessons in *school*. Miz Marvelous lives on the *other side* of town! We've got to think of a way to sneak into that basement!"

"There is no way in this world that I am going near that dungeon," I said, horrified at the idea.

At last we reached Great Aunt Twill's house. Skoot acted out that he'd be in touch later. He acted the way spies must talk to each other, with winks, hand signals, and little beeps. I gave him a beep and a wave of the mitten and raced into the house.

Great Aunt Twill was not happy that I arrived home later than she expected. "It's *after* two o'clock, Little Missy," she said in her raspy voice.

"I'm sorry," I offered. "I tried to be home on time. I really did."

"Where precisely were you?"

"I was with Skoot," I said.

"I didn't ask you who you were *with*, I asked where were you."

"We went for ice cream, like I told you."

"Ice cream? Ice cream? You mean you were at Marvelous Marvels?"

"Yes," I said, taking off my coat and hanging it up on the hook by the door. She sure was forgetting things lately.

"Stay away from that place, and don't tell Lady Mae where you were, whatever you do, not a word," she said.

"Why?" Maybe Great Aunt Twill knew something. Maybe Lady Mae knew something.

She cleared her throat. "I just don't want you going in that place. You could get...*sick*."

She stomped off to the kitchen and I sat down on the floor to remove the boots from my poor frozen feet. I could use a new pair of warm boots, that was for sure.

Lady Mae was at the stove in the kitchen. I had a sort of new attitude toward her since learning she had hard times in this life.

"May I help with the meal?" I said in my most compassionate voice.

She whirled around, facing me. "Help? You want to *help*? You can cook the whole cotton pickin' meal! Here!" And she thrust a wooden spoon in my hand.

I peered into the pot on the stove. "What are you cooking here?"

"Carrot stew," said Lady Mae. "I concocted it with two whole bunches of carrots, and of course, marshmallows. Keep stirring." She plopped down on a chair, pulled out her tobacco tin and stuck a plug in her mouth. Sighing with relief, she sat observing me with her good eye.

I looked at the steaming golden mass on the stove and tried to figure out what to do with it.

"Wash your hands first if you're going to work in the kitchen. That's the first rule of cooking. Did I tell you carrots is in there?" chomped Lady Mae.

"Carrots *are* in there," I said under my breath. I felt nervous with Lady Mae watching me, but after about five minutes, she fell sound asleep, chewing her chaw in her sleep; and I began to move around the room like I was performing a regular kitchen ballet.

I found flour in the cupboard, raspberry jam in the refrigerator, half an old onion, frozen asparagus, and a can of peas under the sink, some peaches. I spread a white dish towel on the table, one without too many spots, and then I made little flowers with my colored pencils and stuck them in a cup in the center of the table as a centerpiece.

Finally, supper was ready and I set the table with a brilliant meal of carrot-peach stew, fried peas with onion, asparagus in butter sauce, 16 raspberry tartlets, and hot cinnamon tea.

Great Aunt Twill and Lady Mae could hardly believe their eyes.

"I think you'll be of some use around here after all," said Great Aunt Twill, and she popped a fried pea in her mouth.

"How in the world did you *do* all this?" wheezed Lady Mae incredulously.

It came to me then, what I had seen in heavenly places.

"I've been to heavenly places!" I announced.

"Er. Did you catch that, Twill?" said Lady Mae.

"I don't believe I did," said Great Aunt Twill.

"It's true!" I said. "Maybe cooking is one of my *gifts*! I've been visited by an *angel* from *God*. An honest to goodness angel! And his name is Harold!" "Fine. Then you say the blessing," said Great Aunt Twill in a fit of laughter.

Lady Mae burst out laughing, too. It was the first time I had ever seen either of them laugh. Every time I tried to interrupt to tell them about Harold and my journey to a heavenly place where I saw the Lord Jesus with prayers fluttering all around Him, they laughed so hard, their tears clinked on the floor.

OK, I got it. No one was going to believe me.

# 13

departm
my m
autl

## Spyii
## May Not Be ~~Good~~
## for Your Health

The next day in school Skoot waited for me at my locker. He talked to me as though we had been together jabbering all night.

"So OK, let's go over the evidence again," he said, very detective-ish.

I gave a sigh.

"What we have here, Bell, is a clear case of child abduction. Do you see it? Martin Menkin's twin sister goes missing and then you and I discover there's a sixth grade person holed up in Marvelous Marvels's basement. You don't have to be a rocket scientist to put two and two together. I say we notify the proper authorities."

I agreed. "Go ahead. *You* notify them."

Skoot looked puzzled. "Right, but *what* proper authorities? We have no authorities proper or otherwise that I can think of in this town. Our police force and fire

ent are mostly volunteer. The town council is
om. Would you consider Riley Rupert a proper
hority? That would be the mayor who doubles as our
chool principal."

"He's the man then," I said. "As principal he would
have information on all the students."

"She," said Skoot. "Riley Rupert, our mayor and
school principal is a *she*, and also the director of the flamenco dancing academy."

"There's a Lake Clearbottom Flamenco Dance
Academy?"

"You bet. We're not total hicks, you know. My
mother has dubbed the town a *Home for the Arts*."

"Come *on*! Get Michelangelo on the phone! Skoot,
there's not even a *bookstore* in town." (I was thinking of
the Complete Works of Charles Dickens I had been
aching to own since fifth grade.) "No bookstore!"

"So? Try the library, dude. ...Who's Michelangelo?"

"Please don't call me dude, dude. And Michelangelo happens to be a Renaissance painter of great
acclaim. Dead."

"Oh? Sorry to hear that." His face went solemn.

"Dead for 400 years," I said.

"Oh!" he said, perking up. "So we won't worry
about trying to find his phone number. Ha-ha!"

We zipped over to Miss Riley Rupert's office to find
out who had been missing from school. She was a tall

lady with hair as black as tar, and she wore it slicked back from her face in a severe, tight bun in the back. Her eyebrows were painted black all the way across her forehead, and she had a voice like a steam engine.

We asked if there was anyone in the sixth grade doing their homework off-campus. Was there anyone absent for a very long time (i.e., was there anybody *kidnapped* recently)?

The answers were nobody, nobody, and no. And what are you kids up to anyhow? A slight blob of mascara had caught on her lower eyelid resembling a black tear about to splash off. She stood straight and tall, her back as straight as a yard stick, and she looked at us like we were two nuts just fallen from the nut tree. Her hands with her long fingers didn't just move, they drummed.

"A couple of families and their children had moved out of town in the last year, but that's it, anything else you want to know? If not, bye-bye, *ciao, arrivederci, hasta la vista*," and she shoved us out of her office.

We left her office more confused than when we arrived.

I told Skoot, "This means whoever is locked in that dungeon is a student at our school! But why didn't Miz Marvelous tell us that whoever is down there attends our school? Maybe even sits next to one of us! Why would that be a *secret*?"

"That's just *it*," said Skoot grinding his teeth like a grownup with braces, "Maybe it's some unfortunate kid she nabbed from another town! Like one of the kids who gets bussed here every morning. I'm telling you, Bell, there is something terribly fishy going on! We've got to find out what it is."

I had such mixed feelings. Here I was, a girl who had an angel visit two times. I, Bellflower Munch, had traveled to heavenly places! Now here I was, in the middle of a kidnapping mystery to unravel? "Listen, Skoot," I said. "I've got a lot on my mind at the moment. For one thing..."

"For one thing what?"

"For one thing..." I stopped myself. There was no time to tell him about Harold and my heavenly journey where I saw prayers answered. I started to suggest we pray together later, but he interrupted to tell me about our test in math, which reminded me I hadn't finished my homework. I promised to meet him at my locker after school.

I had a few minutes before the bell rang, and I knew the best thing to do was pray. That's what Harold had told me to do. I made a dash to the girl's room and situated myself in one of the stalls, the only place I could think of to be alone.

Personal Private KEEP OUT this means YOU Journal

Dear Lord Jesus, first of all I want to thank you for ~~anser~~ answering prayers and for sending Harold* to me. I thank you for the beautiful words he brought me and for the beautiful sight I saw in the heavenly place. I don't feel one bit worthy, but I sure do thank you. Please help Skoot and me save whoever it is locked up in Marvelous Marvel's basement. AMEⓝ

Oh, P. S., please watch over my mother wherever she is and help her not to forget her Bellflower.

And oh, P. P. S., please help me get my MATH homework done so I can hand it in by the end of the day and not get a big ~~FA+~~ F, which will very much upset Great Aunt I will because she already considers me a dunce, which I am not, probably.

Thanks much again.

Love,
Bellflower Munch*,
your child.

After school, Skoot said he had come up with a brilliant idea. (I told you Skoot loved problems. It was like a *calling* for that boy to solve problems.)

# When Skoot gets an idea

# Bellflower when Skoot gets an idea

"Here's what we do, Bell, we sneak over to Marvelous Marvels in the dead of night and break into the dungeon."

"*What? Breaking and entering?* I told you, that's three to five years! One of my mother's boyfriends is still in the pokey for breaking and entering."

"Wow, really? Maybe one day you'll introduce me."

"Oh, you'll meet her. In fact, I'm expecting her any day now. She's coming to get me as we speak probably. She needs me."

"No, I mean the guy in the pokey."

I rolled my eyes. "That's not funny," I said. "And I'm not breaking into Marvelous Marvels's *dungeon.* Count me out."

Skoot thought for a moment. "Say, did you finish your math homework?"

I knew what he was getting at. "Um, no, not exactly. Not at all probably."

"I'll help you!" he offered in a too-chipper voice. "In fact, we can do it right now. You can hand everything in before you leave school and it won't be late. That is, *if* you'll help me at Marvelous Marvels…"

"I hope I'm not going to be sorry," I mumbled as we headed for the school library.

What would Harold tell me to do? I remembered Harold said he couldn't speak anything the Lord didn't tell him to speak. So I'd have to ask the Lord Jesus Himself what to do.

Personal Private KEEP OUT this means YOU Journal

Dear Lord Jesus,
what should I do?
Love, Your child,
Bellflower Munch

I waited that night for an answer from Jesus, or for Harold to come back, but I didn't hear anything and Harold didn't show up. I remembered the vision I saw of Jesus answering every single prayer. Harold told me the Lord wanted me to read my Bible more, so I put on my third grade mittens to keep my hands from freezing off, and reached for my Bible. I read in the first chapter of Luke:

*...Fear not Mary: for thou hast found favor with God and, behold, thou shalt conceive in thy womb, and bring forth a son, and shall call his name Jesus...* (Luke 1:30-32).

The angel Gabriel visited Mary, the mother of Jesus, and told her she'd have a son who would be our Savior! I wondered if Harold was good friends with Gabriel. I climbed out from under my blanket, got on my knees, and thanked the Lord. That's what Mary did. Mary prayed, *"Be it unto me according to Thy word,"* (Luke 1:38) and so that's what I prayed, too.

Be it unto me according
to Thy word, Lord Jesus).
Amen.
p.s. Please show Skoot and me
what to do about the
you-know-what and
you-know-who at Marvelous
Marvel's Ice Cream Shoppe.
p.s.s. Please help Lady Mae
and Great Aunt Twill get over
their troubles and be happy.

I waited some more for Harold to return, but finally went to sleep feeling more cold than ever. Snow blew in the window in the night and piled up on the end of my mattress. I felt like I was sleeping on an iceberg in the North Pole.

In the morning, Lady Mae was waiting for me in the kitchen. "It's about time you lugged yourself out of bed. Did you wash your hands?"

"Yes, Ma'am."

"Good. Let's get started."

She set out flour and baking powder and eggs asked if I knew how to make pancakes. "I'll give it a whirl," I said merrily, and in no time I had cooked up pancakes with raisins, and pancakes with broccoli, and pancakes with marshmallows. We spread peanut butter on them and drank green tea. Lady Mae and Great Aunt Twill were thrilled.

"I declare, a *miracle* has happened in that girl!" exclaimed Lady Mae munching deliriously on a pancake with raisins.

"I should have known," Great Aunt Twill said, "I should have known. It's in the genes."

I felt happy all over. "I guess you might call these pancakes *blessed*," I told them. "Harold told me there are so many more blessings God wants us to have if we would just reach out for them."

"Would that be Harold, the *angel?*" asked Great Aunt Twill with a giggly snort.

"Yes, that's right," I said, and they both giggled and snorted so heartily, they cried. I sipped my tea and smiled patiently at their little moment of hilarious mirth, when who should come bounding up the walk but Skoot. He banged on the back door like he was being chased by tigers.

"Well, let the fool in," said Great Aunt Twill. "Does he think we're all deaf?"

I swallowed a marshmallow and opened the door.

"Bell! I've got to talk to you!" he panted. "Tonight's the night!"

"Tonight?" I gasped.

"Tonight WHAT?" yelled Lady Mae.

"Well, er…" I stuttered. "Um, Skoot has something to do tonight," I answered, definitely not telling a lie.

"Whatever he's doing tonight, you're not included," barked Great Aunt Twill. "You can't go out after dark. That's a rule. *Period*."

"*Period*," repeated Lady Mae.

I pulled Skoot aside to talk to him privately. Lady Mae shouted, "Take off your boots, boy! Don't think you're getting any of these pancakes Bellflower cooked up for us either! If you want pancakes, make yer own! HAR HAR!"

(How unfriendly can you get?)

"Would you like some bugleaid, Skoot?" I offered.

"Well, uh…OK."

He took one sip and his face turned yellow.

Hang on. Did Skoot say *tonight?* Why so soon? Oh why had I agreed to this caper? I knew our motives were good, and maybe we really would help save a life, but still…!

I pulled him aside. "If Great Aunt Twill gets wind of what we're up to, there's no telling *what* might happen to me."

"Don't worry!" he told me. Those words gave me the shivers because I learned back in St. Paul when anyone said to you, "Don't worry," you better start worrying.

That night, without listening to the warning I felt deep inside, I sneaked out of the house. I waited until all was quiet, and then slipped off my mattress onto the attic floor and crawled to the ladder.

I prayed for courage and climbed down as quietly as I could and waited between the mothbally coats in the closet to be sure Great Aunt Twill was asleep. I tiptoed out of the house without disturbing her as she snored and made sounds like a chainsaw.

Skoot was waiting outside for me by the front steps with his teeth chattering in the cold. He carried a bag with some tools.

He told me he had climbed out his bedroom window to make his escape. He could have simply walked out his front door, but what fun would *that* have been? That boy *loved* intrigue.

I spotted his bag of tools. "What are you going to do with those?"

"I'll need my tools to pry open a door or window, S-Silly," he s-said, grabbing my hand. "Come on, we better h-hurry."

"Breaking and entering!" I cried. "Where did you learn about such things?"

"You're not the only one who reads b-books, you know."

"Stop chattering then, please," I said, chattering. "I hope this doesn't take long or they'll find us frozen like popsicles."

We ran along the edge of the road ducking in the shadows of the trees. The sky was full of stars and a huge full moon frowned down on us. When we reached Marvelous Marvels Ice Cream Shoppe, the unmarked truck was parked in back, just like Skoot said.

"That's the truck I told you about," said Skoot. "And look, there's a light on in back of the store. Let's go check it out."

"I don't like this," I whispered. "Someone will see us! Let's go home before we get caught."

"Come *on!*" Skoot insisted. "Don't be *chicken.*"

(If it's one thing Bellflower Munch is not, it's *chicken.*) I followed him, making tracks in the snow around the side of the little building. When we reached the lighted window, it was too high to see inside.

"Here, climb up and stand on my sh-shoulders, Bell, and get a g-good look."

At that moment it was obvious to me Skoot had been watching too many detective movies; besides his teeth chattering was beginning to annoy me.

"Get a *grip*, Skoot, in real life that doesn't work. One of us could fall and break something. And look at you, you're shaking like Great Aunt Twill's Buick in a wind storm."

"We have no choice!" he hissed. "We could be s-saving a *life*. Don't you want to save a *l-life?*"

For the next 20 minutes I tried climbing on his shoulders but I kept slipping and falling off. Finally, he braced himself against the brick wall with both hands and I managed to climb on top of his back and hoist myself up high enough with one foot on his left shoulder and the other on his neck to shift my weight and get a peek in the window.

"What do you see?" he squeaked from below.

"Ssshhh," I said. "I'm trying my best!" What I saw was Marty Menkin, big as you please, sitting on a wood crate box eating a bowl of ice cream. Next to him was a bed with a girl sitting up with a lot of pillows and she was eating a bowl of ice cream, too.

I leaned over to see who else might be in the
room, but my foot got caught on the collar of Skoot's
jacket and I lost my balance. I went flying through the
air and crashed to the ground. I landed on Skoot's bag
of tools which made a sound like rockets going off.
Skoot gave a howl when his head smacked the wall. He
went rolling. The tools went tumbling. I went reeling.

It was fireworks. It was a full orchestra. It was the axe of fate.

There I was, face down in the snow freezing and hurting. Skoot groaned holding his head and trying to figure out which way was up. I heard footsteps coming from the back of the building. I could see the glint of a flashlight on the snow. "Someone's coming!"

I got on my hands and knees and started crawling toward the street with Skoot right behind me. "I think my head is broke," he groaned.

"Broken," I corrected. "You think your head is *broken*."

We stopped short as the flashlight rounded the side of the building and we saw two figures moving toward the truck in back.

"Two people, a man and a woman," whispered Skoot.

"Right. A man and a woman with their arms full of what looks like clothes."

I thought to myself these people must not own suitcases either.

"What did I tell you?" whispered Skoot. "I think we've uncovered a crime ring here."

The man and woman climbed into the truck and we waited for the truck to take off, but it stayed put.

If I didn't get home soon my ears would break off. Besides, for Skoot's information, I saw Marty Menkin and his sister inside Marvelous Marvels having a great old time stuffing themselves on butterscotch swirl.

"Martin Menkin? And his *sister*? You sure it was his sister?"

"Well, you said he had a twin sister. If those two aren't twins my name is Daisy."

Skoot's eyes lit up like two headlights on a hill. I could see his detective brain twirling a hundred miles an hour. "This is better than I thought," he exclaimed. "Oh, it's worth breaking my head for. It's going to take some work to solve this one, all right!"

"Skoot," I said, trying to calm him down, "I don't want to solve anything. It's none of my business if Marty and his sister gobble butterscotch swirl ice cream until the cows come home (from wherever cows run off to). And it's none of my business if two strange people creep around in the snow to an unmarked truck all night every night. I'm out of here."

We pealed back through the trees to Great Aunt Twill's. "We *can't* quit now!" Skoot puffed. He was no longer chattering. "Martin's sister has been gone missing for months. And here she is, right under our noses. I say we have a little talk with Miz Marvelous!"

"*You* have a little talk with Miz Marvelous," I said.

"Bell, would you change your mind if I promised to help you with your math for the entire semester?"

"I'd say we're even since I'm the one with the *English* brains. My fifth grade teacher in Minneapolis said I had *talent*. And remember, you got an A for the poem I wrote for you. Did you know I only got a C for *my* poem?"

He laughed at that one. "Well, how about I promise to teach you to ice skate?"

"Ice skate? Deal," I said, and I knew for certain I'd regret it.

# 14

## Caught in the Act
## of Entering

What happened next threatened to ruin everything. As we got closer to Great Aunt Twill's house, we stopped dead in our tracks at what we saw. Ahead of us, shining in the darkness was the ominous glimmer of light coming from Lady Mae's bedroom window. She was awake!

"OH NO!! What will you do now? Skoot gasped. "She'll hear you come in! You're done for!"

I shrugged miserably. "Great Aunt Twill will kill me soon as I walk in that door."

Skoot started jumping from one foot to the other.

"What are you doing?" I said.

"Thinking, I'm thinking," he said gasping and jumping. "There's a solution to every problem."

I started jumping, too. Anything to keep warm.

"I have an idea!" he said at last, "Let's run around to the back of the house and see if the kitchen door is locked. If it is, I'll try to jimmy the lock with my tools. Then you sneak in, wait until you know it's safe, and then stow away quietly to your room. Simple!"

"Did you say *jimmie the lock*?" I stomped around on one foot. "Skoot, do you realize that is illegal, against the law, forbidden, a *felony*?" It was good to know that the Lord was on his side to protect him from joining the criminal element.

We hurried to the back of the house careful to stay in the shadows. I peered through the window to make sure the kitchen was empty, then I jiggled the door. To my relief and surprise, it opened.

"Great! Problem solved. See? I told you," Skoot said. "I'll see you in school tomorrow, that is if I don't have a concussion, which is all your fault because of your terrible sense of balance."

"My terrible sense of balance! You were chattering and shaking away like Mount Vesuvius about to erupt! How did you expect me to remain balanced?!"

"You're blaming *me*?"

"SSHHHH! I hear something." I held my breath waiting for the voice of doom.

"I'm going h-home," Skoot said with a terrified look on his face, and he took off into the shadows of the trees.

I skulked into the kitchen and clicked the door closed behind me. My feet were too cold to tiptoe, so I took off my boots and left them by the sink. I was sitting on the floor rubbing my toes when suddenly the kitchen light flicked on.

"SO!" boomed Lady Mae, arms crossed on her chest, her face as red as her eyes. Beside her stood an equally angry Great Aunt Twill.

The sudden burst of light blinded me for a few seconds. I tried to speak, but my voice didn't work right. All I could croak was a weak, "I'm home…"

"We can see where you *are*," snapped Great Aunt Twill. "Where have you *been*?"

"WHERE WERE YOU?"

"I've, well, er…I've been to Marvelous Marvels…"

Lady Mae began to wail like a coyote.

"How *dare* you *sneak* out at *night*!" cried Great Aunt Twill. "How could you be so deceitful and so disobedient? Were you with that *boy*?"

"You mean Skoot? Yes, but…"

"Oh! Oh! Oh! Out with a boy!" wailed Lady Mae. "After all we've done for you!"

"Marvelous Marvels happens to be closed at this hour!" yelled Great Aunt Twill.

"It's her mother's influence!" wailed Lady Mae, "Send her away! Send her away!"

Great Aunt Twill ordered me to take off my jacket and bend over. Let me tell you, for a weak old lady she could pack a wallop. She gave me a beating like my mother could never match. I knew I'd have a painful time of sitting down for a long time to come. But even worse than the beating: how was I going to tell Skoot I could no longer be his friend? I was grounded for life.

The next few days seemed endless. I wasn't allowed to leave the house except to go to school. I kept thinking how Skoot promised to teach me to ice skate and now here I was, trapped like a mole and not allowed to see him.

"I'm exhausted," croaked Great Aunt Twill after she had just eaten two helpings of my French toast (which I renamed "Bellflower Toast." Why should the French get all the credit?).

"I'm just plain exhausted is what I am" she was saying, *tired*.

I examined her face. Yup, she looked wiped out. And I was the reason, probably.

"Life has plumb wore me to a frazzle," she said in a weary voice. "I simply have got too much to do."

Too much to do? What did she mean? I did almost all the chores around the house, including spot cleaning the draperies and cleaning under the sink and behind the stove.

"I'm *overworked*," she snapped, as though she could read my thoughts.

I never would understand adults. Adults complain all the time. They love to complain about being overworked. We kids have stuff to do, too, and you hardly ever hear us complain about not having enough hours in the day to do all the stuff we have to do.

In one day alone kids can have a spelling test, a math test, three fights with a brother or sister, get

scolded for being late to school when it wasn't their fault their mother overslept; they can forget their lunch on the kitchen counter, drop their homework in a huge puddle of mud, lose their history book, get ready to audition for the big school musical with a major case of stomach flu coming on—plus all the daily worries like who to sit with at lunch, what's the best medicine to use on zits, how to stay up later, how to get out of doing chores, and how to not get blamed for positively every-thing that goes wrong in the known universe.

With so much on our minds, how come you don't hear us complain about being *stressed out*? How come you never hear us complain about our pressured, over-worked lives? I feel sorry for adults. They just aren't as smart as they should be.

Great Aunt Twill laid a wet washcloth on her fore-head and leaned back in her recliner. "Fetch me a pillow off the couch, Bellflower," she said in a dreamy voice. I did as she asked and placed the pillow behind her head, and as I turned to leave, she thrust her skinny arm out and grabbed my wrist.

"Listen here, girl, don't get any ideas. I'm not dead *yet*."

I could hear Lady Mae in the kitchen clanking dishes around looking for her can of chewing tobacco. It's a wonder that woman didn't chip everything to pieces the way she handled dishes.

Great Aunt Twill held on to my wrist with a tight grip. "You ain't in the will, little girl. So it would behoove you to try to make sure I stay alive. If anything happens to me, you go to an orphanage."

Lady Mae gave a loud cough from the kitchen.

"Don't worry," I said with confidence, "My mother will be here any day to take me off your hands."

"HAH!" she said.

"HAH!" barked Lady Mae from the kitchen.

"And besides, Great Aunt Twill, the Lord won't be taking you to Heaven for a long time." I tried to sound cheery.

"Oh? Don't be too sure about that."

"I'm pretty sure. Harold told me."

"Harold?"

"Harold, my *guardian angel*," I said before I could stop myself.

Great Aunt Twill sat up straight and the cloth dropped from her forehead into her lap. "Are you still on that ridiculous story?"

"Harold is a *real* angel," I said. "You know, like the Christmas carol, 'Hark, the *Harold* Angels Sing.' Harold comes to me in the attic and talks to me. He took me on a journey to Heaven and I saw the Lord Jesus answering prayers!"

(There. I said it.)

Great Aunt Twill looked like she'd just swallowed a big, juicy bug.

"It's *true*," I went on. "Harold comes to me and we sing together, and he shows me wonderful things about God, about Heaven, and about God's will on earth. We're all special! God wants us to take more of His blessings!"

She removed the wet cloth from her lap, gave me her bug-swallowing glare and didn't say a word. Then she pushed herself out of the chair and marched into the kitchen to join Lady Mae. I followed her and kept talking. The words came out fast.

"I know you don't believe me, but Harold told me that the Lord loves us all so much! He loves it when we pray, and when we love each other. The Lord is kind and forgiving and loving. He's here in this room with us right now!"

"I'll have a piece of cheese," said Great Aunt Twill in a hoarse voice. "Or a banana. A cookie. Where are the cookies?"

"You don't do cookies," said Lady Mae.

"Well, we should have cookies. A house should have cookies."

"How about a marshmallow?" said Lady Mae.

"Yes! Good idea! Have a marshmallow. Let's all eat marshmallows."

I kept on talking, fast. "Harold says that God watches over the whole world with love and that He wants to shower us all with His goodness and His blessings…"

"Please stop," said Lady Mae. "You're being a pain in the you-know-what."

"The keester," said Great Aunt Twill. She lowered her voice and talked to Lady Mae as though I wasn't there. "About the orphanage…" she said. "Do they take them when they're deranged?" (*Deranged:* Not right in the head.)

She prattled on about how life had dealt them both a bad hand. She said they got the wrong deck of cards. I didn't know what she was talking about and just chalked her words up as typical peculiar adult talk. What I didn't like was the sound of the word, orphanage. I read stories about those places in books by Charles Dickens.

"I'm no orphan!" I told them.

"Deranged is the word. God has sent us a deranged child," crabbed Great Aunt Twill, "to pay for our sins!"

"I'm not deranged," I protested. "I'm telling the truth and I'm sorry if you don't believe me. Remember, in His time nobody believed Jesus either, and He was the *Son of God*." I excused myself to go to my attic hideaway.

"What about supper?" asked Lady Mae, suddenly bewildered.

"I'll make your supper when it's suppertime," I said. "Please excuse me. I'd like to go upstairs. To pray."

Her mouth dropped open. Great Aunt Twill's mouth dropped open.

"Did you hear *that*? She's going to *pray*."

"*Pray!*" they gasped together like a ghostly duet.

They toddled behind me shaking their hands in the air. "Children are supposed to play with toys! Children are supposed to make a lot of racket, soil the upholstery, break things, cost money, and give everybody grey hair. Children don't go trouncing off to *pray*. Did she say *pray*?"

I left them nattering away and climbed the ladder to the attic.

I leaned on the edge of my mattress and waited for Harold.

"Please Lord Jesus, send Harold," I prayed. "I need him now." My words sounded hollow and the attic remained quiet except for the babbling ladies downstairs and the sound of the wind outside.

"Harold?" I called. "Please tell me what to do! My aunt thinks I'm crazy. If they send me away, how will my mother find me?"

I wrapped my blanket around me and waited. Harold would surely explain things to me. He'd tell me what the Lord had in mind for me. He would see the trouble I was in and help me. Wouldn't he? Help me?

I turned on the lamp switch and opened my Bible. *"Let not your heart be troubled,"* I read. *"Neither let it be afraid. You believe in God and you believe in Me...."* Those were the words of Jesus.

Jesus' words were speaking to me. "OK," I whispered. "I'll try not to be afraid. I'll try not to be troubled. But, Lord, I hope you're paying attention because it looks bad for me. I don't mean to be ungrateful, but could you please give me a little help here? I know You said I was supposed to be a blessing to people. I want to be a blessing, but mostly, I'm a pain in the you-know-what."

I talked to the Lord for a long time. Isn't that what it means to pray? Talking to God? I told him, "Great Aunt Twill and Lady Mae might could be nice folk deep down. (*Might could?* Yikes, I was talking like them!)

"Please, Lord, give those two old ladies big hearts and help them to be happy. After all, You love everybody, right? I believe You must love them enough to help them be happy. God bless them."

Just as I finished my prayer, a huge gust of wind hit the window and shook the entire attic. At first I thought it was an earthquake like the kind they get in Japan. Then it was quiet again. I made little puffs with my breath in the cold air. I could practice whistling or continue praying. I chose prayer.

I started off by praying for the entire town of Lake Clearbottom. I prayed for the people by name starting with A.R., the dry cleaning man, and his dog, Wilbur. I prayed for Martin and his sister. I prayed for Missus *Miz* Marvelous, for Skoot, and for Great Aunt Twill's son, Tellride. I prayed for Miss Kreek, my teacher, and for our principal slash mayor, Riley Rupert. I prayed and prayed.

Then I made a plea.

*Lord, will you please send Harold back…please?*

Silence.

I waited until it grew dark outside. At around eight o'clock that night, Great Aunt Twill yelped, "Bellflower,

# Interesting people of Lake Clearbottom*

Connie McConklin

Me, Bellflower

Skoot

?

*not including Arnold Arkvard

have you *died* up there? Come on down here and make us a little supper, won't you? You don't want everyone to *starve* to death, what with it being so close to *Christmas*, do you?"

I climbed down the ladder and prepared us a nice bowl of steaming potato onion soup and some hot corn muffins to eat with peach jam.

When we sat down to eat Great Aunt Twill said, "Please, could we not talk about angels? That is, could we please not say one teensy word about angels or seeing visions of our Lord. Please?" Lady Mae had her face over her plate smelling the soup. Great Aunt Twill said a blessing and the two of them ate their supper in a state of rapture. If there was one thing they loved, it was eating. Never had they tasted such a delicious soup, they said, never in all their born days.

Lady Mae ate nine corn muffins and they fought over the last one in the pan, which I was saving for my lunch tomorrow.

"I saw it first!" yelled Lady Mae.

"Gimme! Gimme!" yelled Great Aunt Twill.

I took the muffin out of the pan and broke it in two. "Share nicely!" I said like a kindergarten worker.

We ate to the sound of chewing and swallowing and the ticking of the clock on the wall. I couldn't help feel proud when they not only ate thirds of the soup, but they licked up every crumb and drop of the corn muffins and peach jam. My new gift for cooking was the best thing that happened to me since I came to Lake Clearbottom, except for meeting Harold, of course.

But Harold didn't show up that night. And he didn't show up the next day, either.

# 15

## Calamity at Marvelous Marvels

Skoot and I sat at a lunch table in the corner of the school cafeteria where he chomped on a big fat roast beef sandwich and I ate my marshmallows. Skoot's mother packed him the most amazing lunches—roast beef! We sipped our cartons of 2 percent milk. Skoot had been insisting I go with him to Marvelous Marvels to confront her openly. I just knew it was a terrible idea, the worst.

"Aw, come on, Bell, we really must do it. You know, just *talk* to her. Get to the *bottom* of things." He was trying to look cunning. I blew bubbles in my milk with my straw and pretended not to hear him. He was talking in a funny affected voice like a seasoned private eye might speak.

Finally, I looked him square in the face. "Skoot, watch my lips. I'm *grounded*! There's no way I can get out of the house to go confront Miz Marvelous with you. Day or night. *NO WAY*."

"OK, OK. Not so loud. We'll go to Plan B then," he said. "We don't have a choice."

I crunched the milk carton in my hand. "What's Plan B?" I said, nervous to hear his answer.

"We go during school hours."

"*What?* Skip school? If we're caught, what then? I'll go directly to the orphanage without passing Go. No, thank you."

Skoot put his hands up to calm me down.

"Naw, naw. I don't mean skip school, Silly. I'll get us passes at lunch. That's easy. No problem. I'll work it out. Don't worry."

"Don't worry? My life is on the line here, Skoot. Great Aunt Twill wants to send me to an *orphanage*! Are you *listening* to me?"

"Aw, your aunt is bluffing," he said. "Nobody sends a kid to an orphanage when they care for a kid like she cares for you."

I couldn't help but honk at those words. "Skoot, I don't think you've been paying attention to my situation."

"Of course I've paid attention. My mom says she's seen a change in your Great Aunt Twill since you've come to live in her house. She said she's got 'color in her cheeks,' whatever that means."

"That's her new lipstick."

"I'm just saying…"

"Forget it."

He studied my face. "Then it's agreed? You'll do it?"

"Absolutely not! I am not going to trudge over to interrogate Miz Marvelous, no way. Forget it. It's not going to happen."

When Skoot came to my locker with the passes signed by the school nurse, I knew I'd be trudging in the snow to Marvelous Marvels in spite of my vexations.

"It's all official, Bell. Don't be afraid."

That's what Harold had told me. "Don't be afraid, Bellflower," he had said. "The perfect love of the Lord Jesus wipes out every tiny particle of fear in you."

But I hadn't heard from Harold in days. How could I make sure the Lord was with me in this?

I took Skoot by the arm and told him to wait up.

"Why? What's wrong now?"

"We've got to pray," I said.

"Pray? Are you serious? At a time like this?"

"Yes, especially at a time like this," and I broke into prayer begging the Lord Jesus to guide our steps and help us do the right thing.

"Oh Jesus, protect us and lead us to the truth of this whole matter," I prayed.

"Amen," said Skoot with reverence. "And we're not even in church."

"You don't have to be in church to pray, Skoot. You can talk to God any time at all."

A sudden icy wind blew down on us. I kept praying. "Lord, it says in the Bible you are with us always, even forever. And also, You said (which I read this very morning before breakfast) that we can ask whatever we will and it will be done for us."

Skoot called out another big "AMEN."

The street went quiet and all at once I felt scared. As in *chicken scared*.

Skoot let out an exasperated groan. "You are so just like a girl."

"Yeah. Just like."

"Girls are total sissies."

"I am not a sissy."

"Are too."

"Am not."

"Are too."

"AM NOT!"

We arrived at Marvelous Marvels to find the door locked. I wanted to cheer with relief. "OK, we tried," I said. "Let's get out of here."

Skoot shot me a frown and pounded on the door. He pounded and pounded.

"Look over there," I said, giving him a poke. "The, the...*truck*."

Sure enough. The truck we had seen the other night parked in back of the ice cream shoppe was now parked at the side and almost hidden from sight. It had a Christmas wreath hanging from its hood.

"That's mighty suspicious," breathed Skoot.

It occurred to me that we were nosing around in other people's business all because of Skoot's gift for solving mysteries. Skoot was the detective, not me. And here I was, a girl with no mystery-solving gift whatsoever, standing out in the cold, skipping school and risking being deported to an institution.

"I'm out of here," I said.

"You *can't* leave," cried Skoot. "Here's Miz Marvelous now!"

The door swung open with tornado force. WHAM!

"*Well?*" she barked.

We were shocked at her sudden appearance. "Um, er, well Miz Marvelous!" Skoot blubbered, "We just wanted some...uh, ice cream," he said.

"Oh yeah? Why aren't you kids in school?"

"Uh, er, well…"

"For crying out loud, get *in* here, you'll *freeze* out there in the cold." She gave a grunt and pushed us inside "You say you want ice cream?"

"Er…y-yes please." The color had drained from Skoot's face and his voice had gone up two whole notes. He looked petrified.

(Who's chicken now, I ask you.)

"Ha!" shrieked Miz Marvelous. That just goes to prove people love ice cream year round, not just in the heat of summer. What can I get for you?"

We ordered two Chocolate Storm sundaes with tutti-frutti ice cream and extra strawberry sauce, very chocolate ice cream, M&M's, and chocolate sprinkle whipped cream. We looked around the empty shoppe and set our hats and mittens on the counter before sitting down.

Skoot tried to make conversation. "Uh, Mizzz Marvelous…uh, how've you been?"

"You didn't come here to inquire about my *health,* did you?"

She scooped the tutti-frutti into the ice cream dishes.

"Uh, Mizz Marvelous? Just wondering, is that your truck out on the side of the building?"

"Nope," she answered, like that was the end of the conversation.

It was quiet. Then Skoot chirped, "I can see the lights on here in the shoppe late at night. Are you open late at night?"

"Nope," said Miz Marvelous, growing irritated.

"Well then, how come your lights are on late at night?"

She tossed a scoop of Very Chocolate in the dish. "Because they *are*," she snapped.

By the little sneer on her face I could tell she was not taking us seriously. I sat shredding a napkin into itsy bitsy little strips and wondering how it got so quiet. Skoot got more brave: "Miz Marvelous," he said, enunciating every syllable, "I'll come right to the point. Is-there-anybody-living-downstairs-in-your-basement?"

Miz Marvelous reached for a banana and began peeling it. Very slowly she turned to us with the banana in both hands. She pointed the banana at our faces.

"Aren't you just full of questions, little man! I wouldn't be so full of questions if I was you!"

"*Were* you," I said under my breath.

Skoot leaned forward against the counter, his knuckles white. "Miz Marvelous, we believe you're hiding somebody in your basement!"

"You do, do you?" she said between her teeth, still aiming the banana at us.

Strawberry sauce dripped over the edge of the Chocolate Storm dishes. Miz Marvelous took a giant step toward us waving the banana in the air. She tapped our noses with it.

"Don't put your snoots where they don't *belong*! Do you get my *meaning*?"

"Ma'am, we believe you've got Martin Menkin and his sister locked in your dungeon, er…basement!"

(Where did Skoot get all this sudden bravery from? He was just *oozing* with bravery.)

Her eyes grew wide and then she said in a high, creaky voice, "Tell you what I'm going to do. I'm going to serve you your two Chocolate Storm sundaes with tutti-frutti ice cream, extra strawberry sauce, Very Chocolate ice cream, M&M's, and chocolate sprinkle whipped cream, and then you're out of here. No more questions. GOT IT?!"

Skoot didn't get it. "I'm sorry, Ma'am, but I must ask you some more questions."

She grabbed Skoot's arm. "I said no more QUES-TIONS!"

"C-can...can we check the basement?" Skoot choked. (That boy absolutely refused to give up.) I could tell she was hurting his arm.

"*May* we," I corrected under my breath.

Miz Marvelous gave him a nasty grin. "The basement? You want to go down in my *basement*?"

"Y-yes...I mean, well...*Bell* wants to go down there. Not me." he croaked.

Thanks, Skoot. You're a real pal.

I made up a poem in my head and prayed I'd get out alive to write it down.

### What It's Like To Be Afraid

*by Bellflower Munch in her head*


It's a feeling like taking a bite

of something really hot

and feeling it burn your mouth

and your stomach to shreds.

It's like

stepping on broken glass barefoot.

Period.

"Who's Bell? You?' She gave me a one eyebrow up glare. "You scrawny thing? What's with that *hair*?"

(So all right, I forgot to punch down my hair. What's the big deal?)

"I'm Bellflower" I said. "Remember? Bellflower Munch. And I don't want to go down to your basement."

She gave Skoot's arm another painful squeeze. Without another word she served us our Chocolate Storm sundaes with tutti-frutti ice cream, extra strawberry sauce, Very Chocolate ice cream, M&M's, and chocolate sprinkle whipped cream. I stared at mine, but couldn't pick up the spoon.

After about ten hours she leaned forward on the counter and snarled, "What's the *matter*, girlie? What's your name again? Bell Ringer, Tinkerbelle?..."

"*Bellflower* is my name," I said.

"Lost your appetite?"

"No, Ma'am. Yes, Ma'am."

She pranced around the counter and loomed over us, one yellow coil of hair flopped over her eye. "You kids is going to be real sorry you come snoopin' around here!"

(She had the worst English.)

Skoot's tough detective look had vanished. He looked downright scared.

I composed a couple more lines of poetry in my head:

Being afraid

is like trying to get

something painful

out of your eye

or eating ice cream you

just *know* is poisoned. Argh!

What happened next was such a shock we almost fell over on our unfortunate snoots.

A voice came from the direction of the storage room door.

"Hi Bellflower."

We jerked around. "Ohmygosh!" breathed Skoot. "It's *Martin*."

Martin Menkin, thin and pale, stood at the doorway.

"Yo. Hey, Marty," I managed.

He shot me a smile. "Mamma, Bellflower was nice to me at the rink," he said. "I like her."

*Mamma?*

Miz Marvelous stomped her foot. "Honey, you shouldn't be out of bed."

"I want some ice cream, too!"

Skoot and I sat totaled with amazement. We looked like two wooden dummies in need of a ventriloquist.

Marty lifted himself onto the stool next to mine. "You told me you were new here in town, right, Bell-flower?"

I snapped out of my state of shock. "...Right, Marty."

"So how do you like it here in Lake Clearbottom?"

"You want the truth?"

"Yeah. Truth."

"The truth is, it's the weirdest place I've ever been."

He burst out laughing, which brought on a cough.

"Har! Har! OH hee hee. Weirdest!"...Cough... sputter.

Did he need CPR? "Marty, you OK?"

Miz Marvelous rolled her eyes, handed him a napkin. "I *told* you to stay in bed! Now what'll it be? Mocha or pineapple?"

"Pineapple." Cough, cough.

"I happen to think the whole world is weird," he coughed. Then he changed the subject. "Hey, do you like to ice skate?"

"I'm not very good at it, I'm afraid,"

"I told her I'd teach her!" Skoot piped in. He wasn't one to be left out of a conversation.

Miz Marvelous gave Marty a scoop of vanilla with a big glob of pineapple sauce. I knew Skoot was just dying to ask about Marty's sister and what was going on in the basement, and what was hidden out there in that truck.

Miz Marvelous jumped in with, "Tinkerbelle here lives with her aunt over on Lilypad Avenue.

"My name is *Bellflower*, not Tinkerbelle."

"I call her Bell," offered Skoot swallowing his maraschino cherry without chewing.

Miz Marvelous shook the yellow curl from her eye. "And then of course there's Lady Mae," she woofed, "who's no aunt of yours. So how does she take to you, Liberty Bell?"

*Bellflower*. The name's *Bellflower*. Why couldn't she get it right?

I was ready to tell her Lady Mae hated me and it was a good thing we weren't related when my boot caught on the foot rest of the stool and I flipped off the stool. Martin thought I was being funny and howled laughing, which brought on another coughing fit. Miz Marvelous ran around the counter and poured something pink down his throat. Skoot said I had a problem with balance, and he should know.

After Marty's coughing fit subsided, Skoot blurted out, "*Where's your sister*, Martin? Tell us. Tell us."

"Which one?" Marty asked with a wheeze. "My older sister is out in the camper. She and her husband are visiting us from Texas. My twin sister, Marcie? She's back in the hospital. She comes home on weekends."

If I ever felt like croaking it was right then. Skoot's face turned a peculiar shade of purple, and I'll bet, mine did, too. We sat there like two baboons, our mouths unhinged and hanging down to our belly buttons. Birds could have made nests in our open mouths.

"*Satisfied*, you two?" growled Miz Marvelous. "With all the doctor bills, we had to move into the shop here, and it's on the Q.T. because this building is not zoned for residential living."

"You mean the reason your sister went missing is because she's been in the *hospital*?" Skoot gasped.

"Whoever said she was missing?" said Miz Marvelous. "She's sick is all. Sick!" and she started to cry.

I couldn't help myself, I started to cry, too.

Skoot began apologizing like mad and then we were all talking at once and mopping up our tears. I sniffed and bawled like a baby and asked God to forgive me. Our sundaes melted on the counter and we lost all sense of time. Before we knew it, we were late getting back to school.

"Yikes! We gotta go!" Skoot yelped when he saw the clock. "We're late!" I threw on my jacket. I promised Marty I'd come over to see him lots. I told him I'd pray for him, too. I'd pray that the Lord would heal him and also his sister. Miz Marvelous let out a giant sob when I said that.

We were halfway out the door when she vaulted after us. "Wait up!" she shouted, "I think you forgot *this* the last time you visited," and she handed Skoot his Phillips screwdriver from his tool bag. "You left it out in the snow. Better take better care of your tools, boy. You aren't exactly what I'd call broke out with brains."

We stood there like two rats in a trap. "But since my son likes you, come on back and one of these days maybe I'll teach you both a few tricks on the ice, me being a former *professional*," and she closed the door to keep out the cold draft.

I had a feeling like you might have if the ground opened up under you and you woke up in China. Skoot looked totally flummoxed. (*Flummoxed:* confused or perplexed.)

But we had no time to waste. We had to race back to school to try to get ourselves out of the trouble we were in for violating our lunch passes.

# 16

## Starring the Lord Jesus
## in Person

We ran as fast as we could back to school. I left my dumb third grade mittens on the counter at Marvelous Marvels but I managed to get back to school without freezing my hands off. There was no time to go back and get them, being we were already late and in trouble.

Miss Kreek hadn't taken roll yet. I said a big thank you to Jesus as I sneaked into class without being noticed. I slunk down in my seat at my desk, relieved and out of breath. Skoot was not as fortunate getting back to his class. He got a late pink slip and had to go to Riley Rupert, the principal's office, where he spent the rest of fourth period. And he had to stay after school and clean erasers.

I thought about the amazing events of the day (so far). Then I thought about what Miz Marvelous had said about Great Aunt Twill. And why did she ask how I got along with Lady Mae? My mind spun with the odd and mysterious happenings abounding around me.

After school I felt like walking home by myself so I could look at the trees and pray. I wanted very much to be alone and pray for Marty and Marcie, and his family living illegally in the basement of the ice cream shoppe. What I needed was the big wide sky, fresh air, and walking alone with Jesus.

But there sat Great Aunt Twill waiting at the curb in her big old Buick. A big group of eighth graders stood around the car oohing and aahing. I saw Arnold Arkvard who always makes fun of me, and whom I formally hated, admiring the Buick like it was something from gladiator days. Lady Mae was madly shooing them away with an old loaf of bread left in the car from last week.

I'd really get it from Arnold Arkvard now.

"Great Aunt Twill, may I walk home please?"

"Yes," she said, distracted by the crowd of kids around the car. One of them asked for her autograph.

As I turned to walk away, she yelled, "Don't dawdle along the way. And try not to freeze your hands without your *mittens!*"

(That woman didn't miss a thing.)

I walked with my hands in my pockets. What was it Harold said to do? Thank the Lord for His blessings? I wasn't very experienced in the thankful department, but I gave it a try.

I thanked the Lord for His angels, especially for Harold.

I tried to think of something else to be thankful for. I thanked Him for loving me enough to actually die for me on the Cross.

I thanked Him for air. I thanked him for turtles. I thanked Him for my friend, Skoot, and then I broke down and thanked him for Great Aunt Twill and Lady Mae, who couldn't be that bad because after all, they liked my cooking, which was a gift from God.

"Oh yes, thank You for my gift of cooking."

I walked along worrying about how to be thankful when I thought I heard singing. "Harold, is that you?" The singing became louder. Beautiful, sweet singing like I had never heard before anywhere, not even at church in Minneapolis where they had a great big choir and an orchestra of actual violins. Up to now that was the most beautiful music I ever heard.

But this!

The singing seemed to be coming from all around me and above me, and it was incredible. Really incredible! I looked up and there was Harold!

"Harold! Oh, Harold!"

Behind him was a big white cloud. "Bellflower, the Lord has something He wants to show you. Come." All at once I felt myself lifted up and I then was soaring in the sky like the last time Harold took me with him to show me heavenly things.

"Bellflower, look! What do you see?"

At once a field of gold appeared before me. In fact more than one field—fields and *fields*, (plural, lots of them—and all of gold!) I blinked a few times and looked again. I saw not only gold, but silver, and sparkling jewels. The array was endless! I rubbed my eyes at the brightness of it all. It hurt my eyes.

Sparkling jewels, gold, silver, too dazzling to look at very long. It felt like I was looking into the sun.

"These are the blessings I want to give My children," said a voice, not Harold's.

"...Lord? Lord Jesus?"

And there He was. The Lord Himself. Magnificent and gorgeous. I was gliding around in the clouds and then *there*, right in *front of me* was the *Savior of the entire universe!* My hands were warm, my feet were warm, my ears were warm.

My eyes began to sting and I started to hyperventilate.

"Peace, dearest child," said the Lord Jesus, and at once I felt calm as anything. The Lord gave me the most kind smile you can imagine.

(Help. Was I dead?)

"No, dearest, you're quite alive," smiled the Lord.

"Would you like to know the meaning of the vision you've entered?"

I must have nodded or said yes because the Lord began explaining three things to me. "First of all," He began, "The gold, the silver, the precious jewels you see are blessings from Heaven. Second, My children tend to forget all the blessings I have in store for them. Number three, some of these blessings are answered prayers. My children give up too soon when they pray. Often they pray without believing that their heavenly Father will answer. And altogether too often, they don't pray at all."

I felt my nose starting to drip. I really wanted to understand. Would I remember all this?

"I *never* withhold wisdom and understanding from my children," the Lord said. "And, Bellflower, you should know when I say 'children,' I also mean grown-ups. Everyone who calls on the name of the Lord and knows Me as Savior is a child of God. Young or old."

Cool. Old people were *children* of God.

"Pray always. Pray to be filled and guided by My Holy Spirit. Pray and believe your prayers are heard by your Father in Heaven who loves you. Obey My Word and then you will know the meaning of the vision of gold and silver and precious jewels. You will receive showers of blessings."

I sniffed and pushed back the tears. If only I had something to wipe my nose with. I felt so *happy* because never had I dared to even imagine the Lord Jesus personally talking to me!

I blinked my eyes and shook my head. Harold sang out, "Is He not glorious? All hail King Jesus!" Other voices joined him. I felt like dancing, like jumping, like flying! Then the vision slowly vanished and I was smack-dab back in Lake Clearbottom again with a runny nose.

What time could it be? How'd I get there? Had I walked? Flown? Had I magically appeared like some cartoon Manga character popping out of the computer screen?

I knelt down on the ground and choked out, "Thank you…Thank you," because that's all I could manage to think of to do. The Lord Jesus Himself had spoken to me! *Me*, Bellflower Munch, who didn't deserve such a magnificent occurrence, not one bit.

I knew the Lord would help me understand the vision, like He promised. I didn't think He meant He intended for huge hunks of actual gold and silver to come flipping down on our heads, did He? No, of course not. He was using a *metaphor*, just like I learned in writing my poems, right? The gold and silver and jewels *represented* the great *blessings* of God. And these blessings were uh…wh…what? What did I know about *blessings*?

The truth is, I was much more informed about life's troubles than I was about God's blessings! It was quite plain to me now that the Lord wanted people to know a whole lot about His *blessings*.

Personal Private KEEP OUT this means YOU journal

Dear Mother:
I hope you will try to come for me
by Christmas. I've been to heaven and
seen Jesus and I have also had several
conversations with an angel who
lets me call him **Harold**.
I hope you are fine, too.
Your loving daughter,
Bellflower Munch

**BLESSING:**
That which promotes or contributes
to the spiritual and physical
well-being of this WORLD and
the people in it.

**BLESSING:**
To bestow and declare heaven's
influence and divine favor
on the world and the people in it.

**To BLESS THE LORD:**

To celebrate with praise God's
Presence AND goodness.
To LOVE Him totally AND Never
doubt Him, even if your mother
has totally forgotten you.

--Research by Bellflower Munch

# 17

## Can Somebody Please
## Tell Me Who I Am,
## Please?

The first thing I did when I got home was run upstairs to my room in the attic and pull out my Bible. I didn't even take off my jacket. I couldn't wait to read what it said about blessings. In the back of my Bible is a concordance, which is like a subject guidebook. I circled verses in the concordance to look up. Then I wrote them down in my *Personal Private Keep Out This Means YOU* journal like this one in Psalms 68:19:

> *"Blessed be the Lord who daily loads us with benefits."*

How about that? Daily loads us with benefits! Did that include me? I thought about how right from the very beginning when He first created the world, He blessed *everything* He created. Well, He did, *didn't* He? It says so right in the Book of Genesis, the first book of the Bible!

I kept looking up and writing down. I smiled when I found the verse in the Bible that says,

*"I will give showers of blessings"*

in the Book of Ezekiel because that's the very word the Lord used when He spoke to me, *showers.*

My most favorite verses that night were from Psalms 103. You probably know all about these verses, but they were brand-new to me, so I'll tell you what happened when I discovered them. First I read:

*"Bless the Lord, O my soul; And all that is within me, bless His holy name!"*

I told myself right then and there that I would celebrate His goodness, even when things didn't look so hot. I would praise and obey Him, like He told me to do—that is, I'd try to do my best.

*Bless the LORD, O my soul, And forget not all His benefits:*

I stopped right there. Was that what the Lord meant when He said His children tend to forget His blessings? How sad! Heaven is loaded with blessings! They're falling all over the place just itching to get down here to God's children, and that included me, Bellflower Munch.

*Who forgives all your sins, Who heals all your diseases,*

Excuse me? *He heals all our diseases?* That meant He would heal Marty Menkin and his sister, Marcie? I gave out a loud whoop. "They're healed! They're healed!" It says here in the Bible! He heals all our diseases!

*Who redeems your life from destruction, Who crowns you with loving kindness and tender mercies.*

That would be a word for my mother. I felt she could probably use some help and some tender mercy about now. I prayed the Lord would crown her with loving-kindness out there in old sunny California as she searched for her authentic self.

*Who satisfies your mouth with good things.*

Well, that was exactly what I wanted for Great Aunt Twill and Lady Mae. If anybody needed to receive some good things in their mouths it was those two. There were just so many marshmallows a person could swallow in one lifetime.

*So that your youth is renewed like the eagle's.*

And Lord, while you're at it, help Great Aunt Twill and Lady Mae be healthy and strong. Great Aunt Twill talks like she's ready to kick the bucket any minute, and that's just not healthy.

I was in the middle of looking up verses about angels in my concordance when Great Aunt Twill called upstairs, "Bellflower, isn't it time you started preparing *supper*?" I jumped up from the mattress right in the middle of reading out loud a verse I found in Psalms 103:

*Bless the Lord, you mighty angels of His who carry out His orders, listening for each of His commands. Yes, bless the Lord, you armies of His angels who serve Him constantly.*

At that moment I felt very close to Harold, like we were in the same army unit or something.

I climbed down the ladder and started burrowing through the refrigerator for something fabulous to create. "Great Aunt Twill, maybe you should allow me to do the grocery shopping. That way I could plan ahead," I said.

"Hmm," she said looking at me with a funny squint of one eye. "I'll think about it."

I pulled out a jar of pickled corn and a carton of eggs.

"Bellflower, what's that on your face?"

"Nothing probably," I said.

"You look sort of, well, sort of…shiny. Like you've swallowed a light bulb or something."

I handed her the jar of pickled corn.

"Here, hold this," I said. "Are we out of peanut butter?"

"Never mind peanut butter, Bellflower, what is that all over your face?"

I answered as calm as I could. "I've been to Heaven is all."

CRASH went the jar of pickled corn.

"Yes! I've been to Heaven and I saw how blessings are piled up like mad cluttering the place up and people just aren't using them. God's children don't seem to understand all the blessings He has for us. They must not be praying very much, probably."

Great Aunt Twill gave me a look like she had just stepped on a nail. "I just never! ...*never* heard of such a thing! These things just don't happen in today's age...I just *never*...! I just *never!*"

Lady Mae dashed into the room bumping into things. "What is it, Twill? What's the matter? Are you all right? Speak to me!"

She took one look at me and burst out, "What's that shiny stuff all over you?"

"I've been to Heaven and I've seen Jesus," I said and I cracked two eggs into a mixing bowl.

"She says she's been to *Heaven*," croaked Great Aunt Twill. She sputtered and jumped around the kitchen muttering, "*Heaven!*"

"*Heaven*," croaked Lady Mae, whose entire face went south. Her mouth quivered and her eyes bulged out.

"Bellflower," she said, her words dropping like jam from a spoon. "You must admit, taking little trips to Heaven is not exactly normal. Most kids your age do indoor sports this time of year, or they play computer games all day. But *travel to heaven?*" Then her voice got all silky. "...Were you *really* in Heaven? The *real*

Heaven? Like up *there* Heaven?" She rolled her eyes to the ceiling.

"Yes, I think so. See, what happened was, I felt myself get lifted up and then I was in the air and then I saw blessings piled up by the mile and I heard the Lord's voice. Then I *saw* Him!"

"*What? What?* You saw all that? You say you heard the Lord's voice? *Saw Him?* Oh, my heart—Sweet Jesus, this could be the end. An aspirin, someone…never mind. Bellflower, listen here. I'm going to ask you a question. Something important. I want you to think hard before you answer. Did you see…anybody…any *persons*, that is?"

Great Aunt Twill gave out a cry and grabbed Lady Mae's arm. "Lady Mae, sit down! Ix-nay on the alk-tay! Don't say any more!"

Lady Mae yanked her arm away and put her face closer to mine. "Bellflower, honey, did you see…my *son* by any chance up there? Did you see Robert?"

Great Aunt Twill tugged at Lady Mae's arm again. "I said IX-NAY! Don't say anymore! Let her be."

"I'm sorry, but I didn't see any people," I said. "I saw Jesus."

The hopeful expression left her face. Great Aunt Twill crunched down in her chair at the table with a big sigh.

"She's not a medium with a crystal ball, Lady Mae," snapped Great Aunt Twill. "That hocus-pocus business is a sin! Shame on you for asking such a thing."

Lady Mae lowered her head like a child being scolded. "I know, I know," she said in a gurgly voice, "I'm sorry. I didn't want to talk to him, I just wanted to know he's up there."

"Of course he's up there!" Great Aunt Twill said. "He was a good boy underneath it all—and he was baptized and confirmed in the church."

"So who's Robert?" I said timidly. "Or is it a secret?"

"Yes," they said at once.

"Yes what?"

"It's a *secret*. Now that that's settled, can we eat?" Great Aunt Twill brushed off the table with the back of a shaky hand.

"Please tell me," I insisted.

Lady Mae gave a pathetic whimper.

"Oh well," grunted Great Aunt Twill, "I suppose she'll have to find out *sooner* or later. Go ahead, Lady Mae, tell her."

Lady Mae's eyes filled with tears. "Is there any bugleaid? I'll need a drop of bugleaid …."

I poured her a big cupful of bugleaid from the fridge and sat down across from her at the table.

"When do we eat?" she whimpered. "Will we be eating soon?"

I quickly fried the eggs and laid the table with a pickled corn omelet and raisin salad. She took a big chomp of the omelet and cleared her throat.

Great Aunt Twill cracked her knuckles. "Lord, bless this food, amen, and p.s., tell Lady Mae to button it." She dug into the food.

They polished off every last kernel of corn of the omelet and every last raisin in the salad, and Lady Mae started her story. I was all ears.

"My son, Robert, he was a good boy. He got in trouble, that's true, but he was a good boy. He...he started hanging around with a crowd from the Twin Cities. And then he met a girl. He...he was only nineteen when he fell in love with a girl from the Cities..."

Great Aunt Twill jumped up from the table. "I say we pause for dessert. Marshmallows anyone?"

Lady Mae waved a weary "no" with her forefinger. "The girl was beautiful, young, and full of dreams...she wanted to go to Hollywood some day...she, she wanted to be a makeup artist for the stars. I didn't like her right off. I did *not* like that girl. The kind of girl I wanted for my son was a quiet, small town girl, someone with domestic aspirations..."

"What's wrong with having a dream? After all, my mother is an almost-makeup artist to the stars," I said.

Great Aunt Twill slapped the table with the palm of her hand. "Lady Mae, IX-NAY ON THE ORY-STAY. Say no more! Change the subject! I'm going to allow Bellflower do the grocery shopping from now on. What do you think of that?"

"Robert was nuts about that girl," Lady Mae went on, ignoring Great Aunt Twill. "He would have done anything for her, anything at all. He actually up and married her behind my back, oh WAHHHH!"

I could see a huge crying fit coming on. "They eloped!" she bellowed. "How could he? How could he do that to me? WAHHH!"

"Have some more bugleaid, dear," said Great Aunt Twill.

Lady Mae took a gulp of bugleaid, and then another until she had finished two cupfuls.

"Just another drop, dear," she said, "That's it, thank you. OH! My poor boy didn't quite fit into the girl's Hollywood dream, you see. And there she was, a girl living up in the Twin Cities, and Robert living here in Lake Clearbottom. Well, don't you know, he up and moved to the Cities. Then he brings her home and expects me to take to her—well, I *didn't*."

I poured the last of the bugleaid in her cup.

"Then came that night. That terrible night. It…it was a cold night in our beautiful Minnesota, like this one. She sat in my parlor big as you please and she says, 'Robert, I'd sure like me some of Marvelous Marvels's ice cream.'

"I says, 'In this weather? Are you crazy, girl? Let me make you a bowl of noodles, but no, she wanted *ice cream*. She simply *had* to have ice cream. And like I told you, anything she wanted, Robert would get for her, that's how much he cared for her. So what does he do? He hops in his car and drives over to Marvelous Marvels for her favorite flavor of ice cream…"

I jumped up from my chair. "Strawberry Swirl," I said petrified.

"Yes, Strawberry Swirl, it was," Lady Mae said.

I was no longer breathing. "You're talking about my *mother*."

"See…he drove a little too fast. Eager to get back with the ice cream, I guess. There was a crash. He hit Gladys Fleewood's station wagon coming down the cross street broadside. She didn't get a scratch. But he…"

"After that, as a memorial, they put up a traffic light on that corner," said Great Aunt Twill sadly. "It's the only stop light we have in town."

Lady Mae let loose with another sob. Great Aunt Twill handed her the handkerchief from her sleeve. "Bellflower," she said, "say hello to your grand-mother."

I dropped the empty pitcher of bugleaid. Lady Mae was *Grandma* Lady Mae!

"Nobody knew your mamma was expecting a baby at the time of the accident," she said.

"We've been bitter toward your mother for all these years. We blamed your mother for what happened." Now both of them were crying. "It was wrong of us!"

"Wrong of *me*, you mean," sobbed Lady Mae. "I've been horrible, absolutely *horrible*! Poor Florence, raising a child all alone up there in Minneapolis…"

"St. Paul," I said.

"Yes, St. Paul. And me festering away in anger and bitterness! All those years I missed out on Robert's child growing up. Oh boo hoo! Boo hoo!"

They both sobbed so loudly I couldn't think straight. Robert, Lady Mae's son, was my *father*!

"Yes, yes, oh do you think God will forgive us for being so hateful?" howled Lady Mae—who was suddenly my Grandma Lady Mae.

"I…uh…duh…er," my voice came out crackled.

Tears flew everywhere. "Oh, but how could God forgive me?" wept Lady Mae. "I've been a *monster*, a *dreadful* person. I've said terrible things. I treated you and everyone else so *badly*!"

"Jesus loves to forgive us," I managed. "All those blessings and stuff—OH! WAHH!" Never in my life would I be able to keep a dry eye when people around me were in tears.

"OOOOHH!" cried Great Aunt Twill.

"WAHH!" cried my new grandma. (We were a symphony of tears.)

Lady Mae fumbled at her neck and pulled a chain from under her collar. "I feel so terrible, so utterly TERRIBLE, Bellflower; can you forgive me for being so wretched? ...Here, I have something I want to give you...here you are," and she removed a gold cross from the end of the chain.

"It was Robert's...your daddy's. I want you to have it."

I stared at it like it might bite me.

"Go ahead, take it."

I opened my hand and closed my fingers around my daddy's cross. I held it like it was the most precious thing on earth. "My *daddy's* cross..." I murmured. "My very daddy's..."

"And I have something else, too." She rummaged in her pocket, pulled out a wad of tissues, some nickels and a quarter, and key chain with a Disneyland charm. "This was his, too. He never got to Disneyland. Maybe you will, one day." She removed her key from the clip. "Here. It's yours. Now you have something from your daddy," and she exploded in more sobs.

I took the key chain and felt its weight in my hand, Mickey Mouse in a top hat grinning with Cinderella's castle in the background.

There was nothing I could say. I just sat there holding the cross and the key chain.

I excused myself to go to the bathroom. I was curious abut my so-called shiny face, but what I saw in the mirror was regular old Bellflower Munch, and I needed to do something with my hair.

In the mirror was a girl who now had an honest to goodness real dad, even though he lived in Heaven and I would never see him in this life. My dad had a name, Robert, and I was his honest to goodness daughter. I knew who he was and I knew his name. Now that's a blessing.

Personal Private **KEEP OUT** this means
*YOU* Journal

Dear Mother:
The cat's out of the bag. So to speak.
I know who my daddy was, and I
know all about what happened
between you 2. I wish you could
be here for Christmas, but if
you aren't I'm praying for you
anyway. I'm praying for tender
mercies and a nice crown of
loving kindness for your head
from Jesus.
          Your loving daughter,
          Bellflower Munch *

Dear Mother:
     My last letter to you came back
with a big **UNKNOWN** stamped on
the envelope so I'm writing to you
again because maybe something went
wrong at the post office.

you can never tell about those people at the post office who do nothing but look at stamps and addresses all day, they probably get dizzy in the head after just a few hours. Besides, now with Christmas coming, the post office people are probably drained to the gills and can't tell a Mr. from a Mrs. or a street from a lane, a four from a seven, or a zip from a zap.

Please, Mother, answer this letter so I know you are still thinking of your Bellflower and you have not forgotten me.

Signed ME, your daughter,

Bellflower Munch *

P.S. I need a haircut probably.

# 18

## Trapped in Sausages

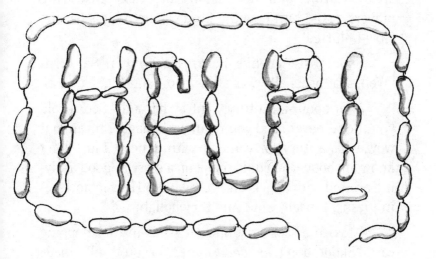

Great Aunt Twill gave me $20 to buy Christmas presents. Lady Mae, make that Grandma Lady Mae, gave me $30 to buy Christmas presents. When Great Aunt Twill found out that Grandma Lady Mae gave me $30 to buy Christmas presents, she gave me $50. I was dripping with money! I was gushing with money! I was a regular money Niagara Falls!

I met Skoot at the Shop 'n Drop. He was waiting for me in the music department where he intended to buy a DVD for his sister, but he decided to buy himself a wiretapping device instead.

I blurted out about Lady Mae being my...well, you know, and I told him about Robert being my dad, and about Harold and my visions of Jesus answering prayers. I told him how the Lord wants to bless people. How I blurted!

Skoot listened like I was speaking in Sanskrit. "Well, that beats all," was all he could mutter.

After about a century went by he said, "See? I told you they'd never send you to an orphanage. I mean, but wow, what a story you came up with! I mean, I just don't know anybody who could make up a story as good as flying around with angels and going up to Heaven and seeing Jesus, I mean, wow. And they bought it?"

I tossed a sack of sunflower seeds in the shopping cart. "Skoot, don't you *believe* me? Do you think I made it all up?"

"Bell, you are a little *different*, you gotta admit. I mean, kids don't walk around talking to Jesus every day."

"Well, they should."

"Huh?"

"Kids *should* talk to Jesus every day. He is so *close* to *us*. If we would just look, we'd *see* Him."

He scratched his ear with his thumb. "I go to church. I talk to God in church. That counts, doesn't it?"

My shopping cart was now almost full—flour and honey for baking, apples, oranges, peanut butter, *roast beef*—"Sure it counts," I said, "But did you ever think the Lord would like a word or two from you during the week? Ever think He'd like to have a *relationship* with you?"

"I dunno," said Skoot pulling his ear. "I never thought of God that way. My dad says church is for sissies who can't handle life on their own."

"Your dad doesn't go to church?"

"He says he needs his sleep. Sunday's his only day off work."

"He doesn't have Jesus in his heart?"

"Guess not," said Skoot.

"What do you say we pray for him right now?"

"*Here?*"

"Sure. We could start off by praying the Lord will shower His blessings on your dad. Then he'll *want* to go to church."

"Don't be a freakazoid."

"I just happen to think we should pray for your dad. Like now."

"But here? In the middle of the Shop 'n Drop?"

"Why not?"

A light went on in his head. Here was an opportunity to find a secret nook to duck into where no one would see us. He was hoping it would be a place of danger. I could see his detective brain working. Maybe we could get into some trouble. Skoot was always a little depressed if nothing spooky happened all day.

"Behind the meat counter!" he gestured, excited. "Look! The butcher's gone."

I wasn't crazy about the idea of praying behind a meat counter, but I followed him and we parked ourselves next to a sink piled with sausages. We started praying for his dad.

"Does this make us fanatics?" he asked.

"I guess."

I told Skoot how Harold had taught me never to *beg* God for a thing, but to *ask* and *believe* that the Lord hears and answers our prayers. I told him how I saw our prayers being answered.

"You honest and truly saw *prayers being answered*?"

"Yes. Well, sure. I think so, probably,"

"That is *freaky*."

Skoot set his wiretapping gadget on the edge of the sink full of sausages and started in praying the Lord's Prayer, which he knew by heart.

Just as we got to "forever and ever, amen," his wiretapping device plopped into the sink and sank between the sausages.

"I'll get it for you," I said, brave girl that I am, and I jammed my arm into the sausages and felt around for the little whatchamacallit. I got my hand down as far as the drain and started poking around in it with my fingers. Once I shoved my hand in, it got caught. I pulled and pulled, but it stayed stuck. It was no use, the harder I pulled, the harder it stuck. I couldn't get it out. My hand was trapped in the drain.

"Skoot, my hand is stuck! I can't get it out."

"Stuck!" he cried, alarmed, "What'll we do we do *now*?"

"Well, what do you usually do when someone's hand is stuck in the drain of a sink full of sausages in the Shop 'n Drop?" I barked.

I could see the glint in his eye. That boy simply adored trouble.

"Don't just stand there, Skoot. My fingers are starting to hurt!"

"Our Father which art in Heaven…" he started again.

When he saw the pained expression on my face, he tried yanking on my arm.

"OW!" I bellowed. That really hurt. The smell of raw pork was beginning to make me dizzy.

"What are we going to do?" He looked dumbfounded, like when Miz Marvelous waved the banana at our snoots.

"PLEASE HELP US, GOD!" He yelled this so loud he surprised even me. At once the butcher's assistant, Ramon, came hopping out of the meat freezer.

"Ugh! What are you kids doing with those sausages?" he demanded to know.

"Just praying," I said brightly. "Not to worry."

"Praying with your arm in our premium pork and veal sausages?"

"So it seems, and my hand seems to be stuck in the drain. Nothing serious," I said.

Skoot jumped between Ramon and me. "Are you a praying man, Ramon?"

"What's that got to do with...?!"

"Do you believe in God?" I twittered, my face practically buried in veal and pork.

"God? Well, sure. Doesn't everybody? But listen here, you kids aren't allowed back here..."

I couldn't stop myself. I asked him if he had ever asked the Lord Jesus into his heart. The butcher!

He didn't know for sure, so right then and there with my arm buried in smelly pork and veal sausage I started praying for Ramon. Guess what. He gave his heart and entire life to the Lord Jesus and asked Him to be his Savior. He was so grateful!

"I used to go to church," he started, "but then what happened was..."

"OK, OK. Hold off on the life story for a while—maybe you could lend a little help here? I'm trapped in sausages!"

"So will you be returning to church now, Brother?" Skoot said, like a regular evangelist. It looked like those two were in for a big discussion.

"Say, do you think one of you *brothers* could help me out here? I'm starting to lose the feeling in my pinkie!"

"I think God sent you guys here today," Ramon was saying.

"HELLOOO!" I screamed.

Ramon looked utterly unconcerned. Like people popped around and got their arms stuck in his sink of sausages every day. He rolled up his sleeves and tugged on my arm until my hand sprang loose.

Clenched between my forefinger and thumb was Skoot's thingamajig.

"Gee, thanks, Bell" he said prying it from me. "You're a real pal."

Ramon was now one happy butcher's assistant, and he gave us each a broiled chicken leg. "Don't worry, they're on the house!"

He said he had been feeling sad because here it was Christmas and he missed his brothers in Mexico.

"Come to our house for Christmas Eve dinner!" I blurted without stopping to think whether Great Aunt Twill and Lady Mae would approve of having guests on

Christmas Eve when they never had guests any day of the year.

Ramon really sparked up. He'd love to come! Especially since he remembered that in the past Great Aunt Twill had never permitted strangers to cross her threshold. When he used to deliver groceries before he began his career as assistant butcher in the prospering meat business, she made him leave her groceries outside on the steps. Was it OK if he brought his wife and children?

I went to the bathroom to wash my hands and my ruined sleeve. Ramon could bring the whole state of Jalisco for dinner for all I cared. It was Christmas! I scrubbed at my jacket sleeve. If Great Aunt Twill saw the mess I made she might change her mind about letting me do the shopping.

But it would have been worth it if I left a finger or two in that drain. Ramon, the butcher's assistant, was now a believer. Heaven was celebrating. I imagined Harold with a big smile on his magnificent face.

I ate my chicken leg like it was from God's own banquet table, one tiny nibble at a time. It wasn't often I got to eat chicken. Skoot gobbled his down in five bites. He got to eat chicken all the time, six days a week when he wasn't eating roast beef, probably.

I told him about my father, Robert, who was Lady Mae's son who died where the only stop light in town now existed. We were standing by the frozen foods section when I told him this, and he turned to me, and without warning, gave me a big fat hug right there by the frozen okra and succotash.

"Oh Bell, you've solved a mystery!" he said.

It was the first hug I received since my mother left for California to find her authentic self.

I spent most of my Christmas money on presents except for the money for my church offering which I folded up in my jacket pocket to take to the service Christmas Eve.

Here's what I bought:

For my Great Aunt Twill: One furry red hat to match her red cape and a game of checkers. (Checkers, to take her mind off her troubles.)

For my Grandma Lady Mae: One pair of cozy new slippers and a Lake Clearbottom poster with the words, Home is Where the Heart is in Beautiful Lake Clearbottom.

For Skoot: A book: *Angels in Our Lives*.

For my mother: The gold cross that belonged to my father. (I kept the Disneyland key chain for myself.)

And for everyone: A Christmas poem by yours truly written on pretty paper with an angel (which looked nothing like Harold) in the corner of the page. Using my clever budgeting, I had money left over to buy food for our Christmas Eve dinner.

Skoot had to get home to help his mother unravel yarn and I made a quick trip to Marvelous Marvels to pick up my mittens. When I arrived, who was waiting at the door but *Harold!*

The sight of him made me breathless. "Harold! Yay! I'm so happy to see you! Oh Harold, it's really you! You're here!"

He was all smiles. I'm telling you, Harold had such a glorious smile.

"Bellflower, dear," he said, "Remember what the Lord Jesus told you. Remember what He showed you." He smiled at me and then all of a sudden he *disappeared.*

I started to panic when Harold disappeared, but I stopped myself. I knew he'd be back. I just knew it.

Miz Marvelous looked up from scrubbing the counter when she saw me enter.

"Oh, it's you, Bell tower," she said. "I suppose you want some ice cream… or maybe you don't. Which is it?"

She seemed tired and depressed. "Well?"

"Thank you, no, and it's not Bell tower, it's Bell-*flower*…I came for my mittens."

"Over there." She pointed to a Lost & Found box on the floor. "I practically nearly threw the ratty things in the trash."

"Thanks," I said. She looked so sad I couldn't help but feel bad for her.

I leaned against the counter and just looked at her.

"Take a picture. It's lasts longer."

I started talking to her. I couldn't help myself. I told her that God had a lot of blessings for her, free for the asking. That is, if she'd like some. She gave a big grunt and swabbed the already clean counter some more with a towel.

"You talk about *blessings*? *What* blessings? Have you noticed all the suffering in this world? You're a fine one to talk about blessings. Just look at you, running around without proper winter clothes with those raggedy mittens."

"The best blessings come to us from within," I offered.

Right at that moment a sweet warm air swept into the room. I wondered if Miz Marvelous felt it, too. I turned around real slow, and there, over by the window, what did I see? Harold, standing there watching us.

"The world is going to blazes in a hand basket," Miz Marvelous was saying, "and you talk about blessings from within!"

Harold was so beautiful standing there watching us. "God gives us strength and hope deep inside us," I told Miz Marvelous. "God gives us supernatural courage." I turned to face her. "I can tell you, I'm much more brave than I used to be since Harold told me how much God loves me."

"You're only a kid. What do you know about anything? ...And who's Harold?"

"He's an angel. He's right here now."

"Sure. And I'm the Queen of Sheba."

"I tell you, Harold is an angel and he's in this room with us right now. I can see him!"

"Only saints and priests who live in caves see angels. Are you better than the rest of us?"

"I'm not better than anyone else—I'm just better than I used to be," I said.

She was quiet and stared at the floor.

"The Lord Jesus showed me He really, *really* wants to shower His blessings on people, and that includes you."

She gave out a sigh. "Listen, Twitter Toes, I was a professional ice skater—are you aware of that natural fact? One of the best. We toured with the Follies, the works. And my twins had so much promise. They were headed for the pro trail, too. But look at the family now! The twins are sick, my ex has stopped paying child support, I don't skate any more, I'm running out of money, and…oh, why am I telling you all this?"

I didn't know what to say. She looked so sad and wounded, I wanted to pat her arm and say, "There-there," like old people and nurses do.

"Let's pray!" I suggested in a fit of inspiration. "Would you like to pray with me, Miz Marvelous?"

"*Pray*?" She gave out a groan, but then nodded her head. "I suppose it wouldn't hurt anything."

She motioned me to take a stool at the counter and sit down. She sat beside me, bowed her head, and folded her hands just like a little child. I prayed for the Lord to *shower* Miz Marvelous and her family with blessings. I prayed He would heal Marty and Marcie forever. I prayed that Miz Marvelous would skate again. I got brave and prayed her ex would pay the child support payments. I prayed in Jesus' name.

It became eerily quiet in the place. Then Miz Marvelous said in a rattly kind of whisper, "Help me, Jesus!" She clenched her fingers together and lifted her head. "I need those blessings within!"

Well, I got goose bumps when I heard that. I looked over at Harold who had a big smile on his face. I felt the Lord in the room with us, too. When you feel the Lord in the room with you it's like taking a bath in light. And you know for sure everything is going to be OK.

Miz Marvelous said, "I feel something. I really do!"

Her face turned soft and she said, "I believe God has heard us!" She never felt anything like it in all her born days, she said.

Me neither.

I was certain God heard us, *absolutely certain*. Miz Marvelous came at me with her arms open and gave me an enormous king-sized hug and cried, "Aw, Tinker-belle! Thanks! Thanks!"

It was the second hug I got since my mother left for California to find her authentic self.

"Could you maybe just call me *Bell*, maybe?"

It was time for me to leave, so I told her to say hi to Marty and Marcie for me, and she said she'd see me in church. I ran all the way back to Great Aunt Twill's with Harold at my side.

He told me, "Good going, Bellflower. Well done."

Miss Kreek read my Christmas poem, which she figured I handed in for extra credit, and said, "Did you really write this?"

"Yuppers," I said. "It's for you."

She smiled with hesitation. "Why, thank you," she said. "Bellflower, you certainly have blossomed lately. Your *attitude* has greatly improved! I don't know what's happened to you, but whatever it is, keep it up."

"Harold happened to me," I said boldly. (I had read that very morning in my Bible how we should be strong and bold.) "God sent an angel I call Harold to me and we're regular partners for Jesus."

Miss Kreek peeked up at me over the top of her glasses and gave me a very teacherly look. "Izzat so?" she said with a lot of throat clearing and neck creaking.

"Well," cough, cough, "such things have happened to others," cough, cough. "There was Jonathan Edwards, John Wesley, John Bunyan, Joan of Arc.... Tell me, are you going to be in the Christmas program at church?"

"No. I was grounded during rehearsals."

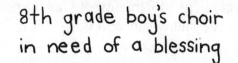

8th grade boy's choir
in need of a blessing

"Oh. That's too bad. Tch. tch."

"But I'm un-grounded now! I can come out of the attic!"

"Out of the—?—well, well."

"Not only that, I can have a friend and I can do the grocery shopping! Isn't that terrific?"

(I was really getting to her. She looked like maybe Martians had landed on the school lawn.)

"You know something, Miss Kreek, or do you prefer MS. Kreek?"

"I, uh...whatever."

I went on like a total idiot. "You know something, Miz Kreek? I never thought I was destined for greatness in the kitchen, but I'm extremely good at peanut butter and pickle muffins, plus lots of other stuff, like fried banana onion bread. And here's a kicker: I don't plan to cook with marshmallows for a whole week!"

She blinked two or three times and twirled a pencil between two fingers. "I seeeee."

I don't know what made me do what I did next, but I hauled off and said, "How would you like to come to dinner at our house on Christmas Eve?"

She was shocked. "Oh! Your house? How nice. I don't know, well, oh, goodness me, OK, yes, yes, Bell-flower, I'd like that. *You* won't be cooking, of course. Heh heh, will you? Thank you. Thank you very much for inviting me."

It was settled. My teacher, who never cared two beans about me, was coming over for Christmas Eve dinner, which of course, heh heh, I *would* be cooking.

"Well, aren't you the little missionary," said Great Aunt Twill when I told her I had invited a few folk for Christmas Eve dinner. "Shouldn't you have asked my permission, being it's my house and all?"

I was ready to start worrying when Lady Mae piped up, "I say it's about *time*!" she hollered. "Yes, Twill, It's about time we had some *human congress* in this place! We've been holed up here alone and miserable long enough!"

Her voice went sweet and she turned to me with her eyes big. "Now tell us, Bellflower, dear girl, what do you plan to serve everyone eat-wise? Something incredibly yummy-wummy delicious, I suppose?"

"Tradition has it that we eat fish on Christmas Eve," announced Great Aunt Twill in a nicer-than-usual voice.

Oh? Fish? Maybe I shouldn't have been so confident about my new calling as a cook. The only fish I tasted were the tuna salad sandwiches from the cafeteria at my old school in St. Paul.

"It's a secret," I said.

I got a flash of an idea right then. "I've got to go out for a little bit," I said, "but I'll be back before it's dark, I promise."

"But what about our *supper*?" cried Lady Mae. "You can't leave. You're grounded. Isn't she grounded, Twill?"

"I can't remember. Is she?"

I left them to figure out my state of being, assuring them I'd be back in time to prepare their supper. Maybe they could nibble on the potato salad in the fridge until I returned.

Outside it had started to snow and on Main Street I could hear Christmas music playing.

*Here comes Santa Claus,*

*Here comes Santa Claus,*

*Right down Santa Claus Lane...*

I walked along in the falling snow toward Marvelous Marvels. How I used to wish Santa Claus would bring me something I wanted for Christmas, like the complete works of Charles Dickens or a laptop of my own, but every year I received something like hard-hold gel for my crazed hair, or a new pair of sneakers, practical stuff. Sometimes I'd get a couple dollar bills or a game like Monopoly, which took too long to play and my mother always quit if I bought Boardwalk, even if she owned Pennsylvania Avenue and all the utilities.

I walked through the door of Marvelous Marvels and was in the middle of thinking about the blessings God wanted to pour out on His children when who should come bounding up from the basement but Martin Menkin.

Yes, *bounding*.

"Wow, Marty! You look positively *normal*," I exclaimed, surprised as all get-out at how good he looked, and wishing I hadn't used the word normal, since it was something nobody ever considered I was.

"The new medicine is working!" he said. "I feel great!"

New medicine? I wanted to dance for joy. I wanted to sing, play a harp, bang on a tambourine. Marty felt great, and the name of that medicine was Jesus.

"And Marcie? How is she?"

"She's coming home from the hospital tomorrow. She'll be home for Christmas. The doctor said he can't figure it out, but she's made a complete turn-around.

Talk about blessings.

"The Lord hugs our prayers," I exclaimed, not knowing what else to tell him.

I invited them all to our house for Christmas Eve dinner. Miz Marvelous was genuinely touched at the invitation.

"Of course we'll come! Your Great Aunt Twill and Miss Lady Mae haven't spoken to me in a lot of years. If they're ready to bury the hatchet, so be it."

"The accident wasn't your fault," I said.

"No, but they've blamed me all these years. Me and his girlfriend's love of ice cream."

"That girlfriend was my mother," I said.

Her face went soft and she blew the coil of hair from her eye. "So they finally told you."

"Yes, and I'm all right with it now," I said.

"As for me, honey, I want you to know I liked your mother. She was a perky kind of gal. Pretty. Everyone liked her. Except Lady Mae, naturally. Nobody was good enough for her son. I can't figure out why you got such a goofy name, but be that as it may. People is peculiar."

(Are peculiar, I thought. People *are* peculiar.)

On my way home I prayed about how to tell Lady Mae and Great Aunt Twill that Marvelous Marvel and her family would be joining us for Christmas Eve dinner, too. What if deep down they still held a grudge against her? I remembered the words from the Lord's Prayer: "Forgive us our trespasses as we forgive those who trespass against us...."

And the Bible verse, *"Casting all your cares upon Him because He cares for you...."*

I stood under the big green wreath hanging from the lamp post in front of A&R Dry Cleaners and took a pitcher's stance. First the wind-up and then the pitch! Z-I-I-NG went my cares as I cast them on the Lord who could handle them a whole lot better than I could.

Mr. A.R. gave me a worried wave from the door of his dry cleaner shop. "Whatever you're pitching, don't break a window!" he yelled. "Baseball season is in the fall!"

I waved back. And Jesus is forever.

## Bellflower's Christmas Poem
*by Bellflower Munch*

The angels celebrated in the sky
on the first Christmas Day
and they had lots of reason to sing
and be happy because they knew

what the world can't take in. How
can anyone born of human blood
grasp never-ending goodness and life
eternal when it's so much easier

to suffer? Harold, my angel celebrated
that day with his friends in heavenly places,
and he goes on singing, because he lives
in the presence of God. I live in the presence

of God, too, and ever since I went to heaven
and saw His blessings rushing toward us here
on the earth I don't have to remind myself to
love Him back. I see Him in you.

# 19

## Christmas Eve  Like No Other

Great Aunt Twill drove us to church at 10 in the morning for a pretty candlelight service (in broad daylight) with the altar loaded with red and white live (not the plastic kind) poinsettia plants and a ten-foot Christmas tree, and wreaths all over the walls. Connie McConklin, the most perfect girl in sixth grade, sang "It Came Upon a Midnight Clear" while Tomlin Ork played the piano. The congregation sang "Silent Night" followed by "Oh Little Town of Bethlehem" and "Oh Come, Oh Come Emmanuel;" then a tenor from Duluth got up and sang "O Holy Night," and I mostly sat worrying about my roast beef in the oven in the pan with a king salmon, and looking around for Harold.

Pastor Schlinmbim preached a sermon on how Jesus came into the world to bring us joy instead of sorrow, victory instead of failure, and healing instead of sickness, prosperity instead of lack and poverty. He said Jesus promised we'd never be lonely because He said, *"Lo, I am with you always,"* and besides that, He would never stop loving us because that's what we were created for—to be loved by Him and to love Him back.

I burst into applause, and Great Aunt Twill gave my arm a slap. But then a few more people started clapping and pretty soon everyone in the church was clapping like mad.

"Amen! Come on!" shouted Lady Mae.

I looked around and saw Skoot sitting with his mother and sister and right next to his mother with his hair slicked and shiny and wearing a shirt and tie was his dad! Skoot mouthed, SEE YOU AFTER OUTSIDE. IMPORTANT.

(What nutty plot did he have on his mind this time?)

I saw *Miz* Marvelous, Marty, Marcie and who must have been the older sister with her husband, each wearing big smiles on their faces. And there was Ms. Kreek with Riley Rupert, our principal.

I saw A.R., the dry cleaner, and about ten kids from my class at school, including Arnold Arkvard. He gave me a little wave with his fingers and then pointed to his head and stuck his tongue out at me.

Cute, Arnold.

I recognized almost every person sitting in that little Lake Clearbottom church on Christmas Eve. In all the places I had lived, I never got to know more than about two people at a time. Yup, the blessings were flying down like crazy.

(Forget Arnold.)

Pastor Schlinmbim preached his message telling everybody we should never allow ourselves to feel defeated, bitter or hateful because these emotions will just ruin the joyful lives we were meant to live. As I sat listening I saw something move behind him. A ray of light. Then I saw a figure take shape in the light. That figure was *Harold*! I saw him plain as day! He had his arms around the pastor and was whispering in his ear.

"LOOK! LOOK! It's Harold!" I whooped, grabbing Grandmother Lady Mae with one hand and Great Aunt Twill with the other. "Do you *see* him? Do you *see* him?"

"Shush now, *shush*," whispered Lady Mae. "That's just Pastor and the poinsettia plants."

I was so happy to see Harold, I could have cried, and I did. Two big tears balanced on the end of my nose and stayed there, and once again I didn't have a hankie on me. I was transfixed at the beautiful sight of Harold as he stood whispering in Pastor Schlinmbim's ear.

"Our little town is a blessed town," thundered Pastor Schlinmbim, "and if we choose to love God His way we will be blessed indeed!"

*You tell 'em, Reverend!*

When the sermon ended, we all clapped again and rose to our feet and sang "Joy to the World" like we meant it.

I was so excited at seeing Harold in church I could hardly concentrate on preparing my big Christmas Eve dinner. I had invited practically the whole town! The first people to arrive were Skoot and his family. Skoot's mom bustled into the kitchen and looked around. "My, you people could use some hand-embroidered towels, I see." Then she said, "Who's doing the cooking?" When she saw I was the only one scurrying around mixing and

chopping and frying and boiling and baking, she cried, "My goodness, you, Bellflower?"

"You got that right."

"Well, uh, might I help with anything? That's what we women usually do at a gathering where food is served. We go to the kitchen and ask if we might help with anything. So what do you say, dear? Might I help, say, perhaps mash the potatoes?"

Mash the potatoes? "No, thanks," I said cheerily. "We're not having potatoes. We're having boiled eggs. So much more substance to them than potatoes, don't you agree? Boiled eggs and gravy. Yum." I thought for a moment. "But then again, I'm not very good at gravy, so make that peanut butter. Boiled eggs and peanut butter."

Her smile vanished.

Here's the thing about cooking: You take individual elements, mix them together with certain other elements, apply heat, and *presto*, you've got something tasty. Then you put these lovely elements on a plate or in a bowl and you arrange the colors, the textures, the tastes, and you've got something even more exciting to the palate. Parsley, for instance, seems more green when you pile some on a plate of boiled eggs. Peanut butter, of course, goes with everything.

And then there are marshmallows.

Skoot's sister, Tamara, saw me working in the kitchen and said, "Like I am so totally *sure*." She looked me over. "Like your hair is like so like totally cool. How *do* you do that? Are those extensions?"

Oh oh. I forgot to mush my hair down. It probably looked like the Amazon jungle, probably. But here was cool Tamara, a *tenth* grader, talking to me. Oh, life was good.

Great Aunt Twill had set up extra tables in addition to her big dining room table, and Lady Mae brought out all the best china and silver, and extra napkins and lots of chairs.

Counting Ramon and his family who flew in from Mexico and four cousins; Pastor Schlinmbim and his family of eight; A.R., the dry cleaning man and his standard poodle; Marvelous Marvel and her family; Skoot and family; the Sunday School director and family; Ms. Kreek; our principal, Riley Rupert; Mr. Pettlefry, the postman and family; Great Aunt Twill; my Grandma and me, we were a jolly crowd.

Here's what we ate: roast beef and pickles, baked salmon and lemon sauce, walnut cranberry salad, fried string beans, lettuce cups filled with marshmallows, boiled eggs with peanut butter gravy, peaches and pear yogurt, date nut biscuits, tomato basil onion soup, and my crowning achievement, baked Ovaltine strawberry ice cream peanut pie with little candy canes poking off the top. And to drink: bugleaid, which we all drank several glasses of. Tamara, Skoot's cool tenth grade sister, thought everything was simply *fab*, and ate three helpings of peanut butter gravy.

After dinner when we all sat burping and grinning at each other, Skoot said he had to speak to me ASAP in private. It was urgent. I told him whatever it was, it would wait. Couldn't he see I was basking in acceptance? All I wanted to do was sit back in my chair and gaze at the contented faces who enjoyed my cooking.

"The best Christmas Eve feast I ever ate," said A.R., the dry cleaner, dropping a date nut biscuit to the floor for his standard poodle.

"I've never spent a more wonderful Christmas Eve," said Ms. Kreek.

"We certainly are blessed that Bellflower came to Lake Clearbottom," said Pastor Schlinmbim crunching on a candy cane.

They all cheered at that, but I thought no, we're really blessed that *Harold* came to town.

*"Bless the Lord, you armies of his angels who serve him constantly"* (Psalm 103:20). Bless the Lord, Harold, and bless the Lord oh my soul, too.

Somebody hollered out, "Give us a dance, Twill!" And to my utter astonishment, my Great Aunt Twill rose to her feet and called forth Riley Rupert who said, "We missed you in class last week, Twill."

*"Arriba! Arriba!"* crowed Great Aunt Twill.

*"Flamenco!"* cried Riley Rupert, parading to the middle of the floor and striking a pose.

*"Flamenco!"* cried the crowd. A.R. clinked his glass with his fork.

*"Andalay!"* cried Great Aunt Twill, and my otherwise sickly great aunt began stomping and snapping her fingers as Riley Rupert sang and clapped and everyone cheered and clapped along with her. Great Aunt Twill clicked her heels and danced around the room like she was personal friends with the famous Jose Greco.

Skoot kept trying to get my attention and I kept giving him the eye to stop bothering me. Couldn't he see this was a momentous occasion? If only I had a camera.

It was much later when he caught up with me in the kitchen as I was bringing more bugleaid to our happy guests.

"I must talk to you, Bell, in private! I must!"

"OK, but make it quick," and we ducked into the broom closet for privacy.

"It's about your mother."

"My mother."

"See, I found out your mother and my mom used to be friends. At least they knew each other way-back-when. My mom, as you may not know, quit beauty school to take up the cross stitch…"

"OK. And…? *And*?"

"See, your mother called my mom on the phone from California. She didn't want to call your great aunt or Lady Mae because she didn't want any hassle."

"What did she say? What did she say? Is she coming to get me?"

"No."

"NO? *NO*?"

"No."

"But how come? She's not sick or hurt or anything, is she?"

"I don't think so."

"And she's *not* coming to get me?"

"Like I said, no, she's not coming."

"Don't tell me anymore, Skoot! I don't want to hear it."

"But there's a reason, Bell."

"I don't want to hear it!" I tore out of the broom closet and fled to my room in the attic where I parked myself on the floor with my *Personal Private Keep Out This Means YOU* journal.

I wrote:

*what they have been saying is* **TRUE** *after all . my mother isn't ever coming for me .*
## THE END

But of course, it wasn't the end. Nothing is ever the *end* end. Things always continue on, like time that stops for no one.

I woke on Christmas morning and made the decision to be brave. I would face my woes with courage, like Harold told me to do, and like Jesus told me to do. I put on my one and only dress and climbed down the ladder to the living room where Great Aunt Twill and Lady Mae were sitting in their chairs waiting for me.

"Merry Christmas!" they caroled.

"Merry Christmas," I said, arranging the best smile I could on my face. I discovered presents under the tree for me and I opened them to find a new jacket with a hood and fleece lining. And next to the jacket was a pair of shiny white ice skates. I wanted to be happy, I really did. I gave both Great Aunt Twill and Lady Mae a big kiss on their cheeks.

"Call me Grams from now on," said Lady Mae. "Won't you? Please?"

"OK, Grams," I said.

"Right after Christmas we're taking you to the Shop 'n Drop and buying you a whole new wardrobe, including mittens."

Practical stuff.

"Here's one more…" and Lady Mae handed me a box with a pair of new shoes inside.

They opened their presents from me and were so happy doing it, I almost felt embarrassed. "These are the best presents ever!" they said.

I could hear the big clock ticking in the parlor. "Bellflower, we are so happy and blessed you came to live with us. We want you to know, well, we are glad. And, well, we love you."

The only person I had ever said "I love you" to was my mother. Now here I was, feeling very much like I loved Great Aunt Twill and Lady Mae—oops, *Grams*, too. But maybe if I loved them too much, they'd leave me, too. All I could say was yup, and wring my hands.

We sat down to eat our breakfast, which happened to be leftover baked Ovaltine strawberry peanut pie.

"Boy, those people last night sure did chow down Bellflower's cooking, didn't they, Lady Mae?" said Great Aunt Twill.

"Nary a crumb left, and it's all to your credit, Bellflower," she answered. "Bellflower, you have a mighty gift for cooking, that's for certain. I almost bought you a cookbook but you don't seem to need one!"

I mustered up a smile. They had cleaned the kitchen spotless, even scrubbed the pots and pans, which was usually my job. They ate two pieces of pie each. I couldn't finish mine. It reminded me of my mother's favorite, Strawberry Swirl.

Great Aunt Twill and Grams wanted to linger on about how wonderful our Christmas Eve had been, how blessed they were with the food, the prayers, the flamenco dancing, the singing.

"Singing? Did I miss the singing?" I asked.

"Oh yes, "The butcher's wife brought her autoharp and we sang all the verses of "Silent Night" in Spanish! I'm surprised you didn't hear us. Oh, you must have been sound asleep."

"Yes, dear, you worked so hard preparing such a grand feast. Oh, and grand it was, praise the Lord."

It occurred to me that Great Aunt Twill had stopped complaining about being tired and exhausted. And she had danced the flamenco! I watched those two old ladies who said they loved me as they chattered away, and I thought how important it was to hold onto happy moments.

Their laughing and re-living the events of last night was how they held onto their happy moments, and I prayed God would give them lots more. Me, I would always be around to cook their suppers, probably.

Personal Private **KEEP OUT** this means *you* Journal

Bellflower's Boiled Eggs With Peanut Butter Gravy

(Serves 4)
4 eggs
½ Cup creamy peanut butter
½ Cup regular milk (or coconut milk if you have some around)
1-½ teaspoon curry powder
1 teensy dash chili paste

Fill a pan with water just enough to barely cover the eggs and bring to a boil. Lower the heat to a smiling simmer and lower the eggs into the water. Don't worry if they crack because you'll be taking the shells off later. Boil for **10** minutes until you have hard boiled eggs.
Remove from the heat and run cold water over them.

Peanut Butter Gravy:
In a small bowl mix together the peanut butter, milk, curry powder and teensy dash of chili paste with an electric mixer. Peel the eggs and slice them in rows on a plate. Spoon the peanut butter gravy down the center of the eggs.
Scrumptious!!
You can also spread this yummy gravy on toast or biscuits or apples or even MARSHMALLOWS!

# 20

## Does Anybody Here Believe in Miracles?

Later Christmas afternoon Great Aunt Twill and I played about 16 rounds of checkers because she insisted on playing until she won a game. "It's not easy living with such a little genius," she said, frustrated. "Bell-flower writes poems, she cooks, she wins at checkers. What will she excel at next?" I knew she was doling out the compliments in an attempt to cheer me up. I was in a sullen mood and I'm afraid I wasn't doing a good job of hiding it.

"Have you noticed anything different about me?" Lady Mae said.

"You're not chomping on chaw, are you?" said Great Aunt Twill appreciatively.

"Nope. I gave it up. I cold-turkeyed it."

Great Aunt Twill and I both gave a cheer. "We're proud of you," we said.

"I'm proud of me, too," said Lady Mae. "We come from a long line of chawing kin."

At around five o'clock, the time Great Aunt Twill liked to take her vitamins and start asking about supper, there came a knock on the front door. Usually people rang the bell, but this time whoever it was knocked instead of ringing.

"You answer it, Bell."

Standing in the snow with ice skates slung over their shoulders and pulling a sled was Marty Menkin and his sister, Marcie. "We're on our way to the rink, but we had to stop by and thank you for all you've done for us," said Marty.

"And we brought you a present," said Marcie.

"Well, don't just stand there in the cold, children, come on in!" shouted Lady Mae.

Marty and Marcie sheepishly entered and Lady Mae led them into the parlor with their boots traipsing snow and all. "It's good to see you children," she extolled.

"Thank you, Ma'am," said Marcie politely. "We came to tell Bellflower that our mother, the former

'Miss Marvelous On Ice' is so happy about the blessings of the Lord that she's named an ice cream flavor after her. She's calling it *Bellflower Surprise,* and we brought four hand-packed gallons on our sled for your freezer."

She got my name right! I couldn't have been more shocked if a town had been named after me. We carted the gallon containers to the kitchen and jammed them in the freezer.

The doorbell rang again and Ms. Kreek entered to announce she had a present for me, too. "You've made quite an impact on the town of Lake Clearbottom," she said, and so I'd like to give you a little present." She handed me a package wrapped in silver paper. I opened it with Great Aunt Twill and Grams beaming alongside me. It was a silver angel figure!

What could I say? The angel figure was female with long (straight) blond hair and *wings.* Harold didn't have wings and he wasn't a lady with long straight blond hair. He was big and strong and his hair was dark and wavy. He had the kind of face you could trust, although I couldn't exactly describe it.

I set the figurine on the piano and thanked her.

"I say we eat some of that Bellflower Surprise ice cream!" cheered Grams.

Marcie wanted to know if I *really* had seen an angel.

"Yes, really," I told her, even though inside I was beginning to be afraid he might not show up again.

"That is so *cool*," gushed Marcie, who, by the way, looked so healthy you would never know she had been abiding at death's door.

I brought out bowls for everyone when the doorbell rang *again*.

A stranger stood in the door, a man I hadn't seen in Lake Clearbottom. A handsome man he was, dark curly hair, a wide smile.

"Merry Christmas," he said.

"Merry Christmas to you, too," I said.

At the sound of his voice, Great Aunt Twill came flying out of the kitchen.

"TELLRIDE! My TELLRIDE! You came home!" and they were in each other's arms hugging and laughing and crying all at once.

"Look who's here, everyone! It's my Tellride!" and she hugged him some more.

Lady Mae came reeling out of the kitchen too, and threw herself at Tellride. "Oh dear, dear boy!" she cried. "Dear, dear boy!"

It was, to say the least, a most dramatic moment.

But breaking the intense emotion of this scene came A.R., the dry cleaner with his standard poodle. "I was out walking Wilbur and I had to stop by to thank you," he said, and spotting Tellride, he said, "Well, what do you know, it's Tellride! Where have you been, boy? You haven't picked up your pants. Two pairs."

"We've missed you so much!" screeched Great Aunt Twill. "Oh Tellride, can you forgive your mean and previously vindictive mother? I've changed, my darling son, I've changed!"

"Well, don't just stand there, Tellride. You too, A.R., come on in! Bring the dern dog, too!" called Grams. (I was dumbfounded she wasn't concerned about the carpet.)

So A.R., the dog, and Tellride pulled up chairs in the kitchen with Ms. Kreek, Marcie, Marty, Grams, and Great Aunt Twill.

I set out bowls for everyone to sample Bellflower Surprise ice cream. I took my time opening the ice cream container to prolong the suspense. What flavors were to be known for all posterity as Bellflower's Surprise? I opened the ice cream carton and scooped a spoonful and handed it to Lady Mae.

"You be the first to taste it," I offered.

She took the spoon, licked, savored, swallowed. The flavor? Peanut butter-marshmallow!

"Hear hear!" cheered Great Aunt Twill.

"Woof," said Wilbur.

We were about to say a blessing and dig into the ice cream when the doorbell rang again. Skoot and his whole family stood outside in the snow.

"You're just in time for ice cream! Bellflower Surprise ice cream!" shouted Great Aunt Twill.

They filed into the kitchen and Skoot grabbed the sleeve of my sweater. "Wait a sec," he said. "I haven't given you my present yet." He took my hand and led me to the front door.

"I don't want to go anywhere, Skoot. I want to stay here."

"Hang on," he said. "You're not going anywhere." He flung open the door.

The sun was setting and a soft golden glimmer fell over the snow. There, with the sun behind her beautiful head stood none other than my very own mother.

She threw open her arms. "I missed you so much, Flower!" I was suddenly smothered in her fur and Chanel Number 5 cologne.

"I drove three days and nights to be here by Christmas," she was saying. "Let's have a look at you! Oh goodness, that hair! Never mind, I've got a new conditioner. Oh, give us another hug!"

I was so happy to see my mother, I couldn't think straight.

"Skoot arranged for me to surprise you," she said brightly.

"But Skoot said you weren't coming."

"How could I be coming when I was already *here*?"

Lady Mae came rushing at my mother and nearly knocked her over with hugs. "Oh dear dear girl, forgive me, forgive me!"

There ensued quite an emotional scene with everyone hugging and kissing and saying thank you to God.

We ate several bowls of Bellflower Surprise ice cream and I thanked the Lord for the best Christmas ever.

The sun had set and the sky was dark. Someone began singing, "Hark the Herald Angels Sing." We were singing away and waving our spoons in the air when I happened to glance out the window. Who did I see high in the sky over the town of Lake Clearbottom singing with a host of other angels but *Harold*. He was singing full blast with so much joy, "GLORY TO THE NEW-BORN KING!"

"Look! Look!" I cried. "Listen!" Can you see him, can you hear him?

By the stunned expression of everyone's face, I knew they saw Harold as clearly as I did, and they heard the choir of angels, too.

"...JOIN THE TRIUMPH OF THE SKIES," they sang. We all dropped our spoons and napkins and ran outside in the snow singing:

WITH ANGELIC HOST PROCLAIM

CHRIST IS BORN IN BETHLEHEM!

HARK, THE HAROLD ANGELS SING,

GLORY TO THE NEWBORN KING!

It was late Christmas night when our guests left for their own homes in various states of joy and astonishment. We had all seen and heard angels singing! We would never be the same after being in the presence of angels. Oh, heavens! We had *sung with the angels*.

The lights of the town of Lake Clearbottom twinkled happily and the night air was fresh and clean, as though swept with a heavenly broom. Grams held my mother in her arms kissing both her cheeks. "I lost my son, but I don't want to lose you again, dear girl. That is, if you'll *forgive* a selfish old lady, and consent to being the daughter I always wished I had."

"Why not?" said my mother. "I've been pretty selfish myself. Will you forgive me, too?"

And then she said something Grams didn't know. "When Robert and I eloped," she said, "we planned on making our home here in Lake Clearbottom. We were going to tell you that night when the accident happened and, well, I couldn't stay here after that with all the hostility toward me and what with my own bitterness and grief, I felt I had no choice but to go to the Cities."

Grams hugged her again and broke into a new flood of tears.

"I brought Bellflower here to stay with you," my mother continued, "because I hoped maybe you'd learn to like her in spite of the fact that she's my daughter."

Tears and hugs and more tears and hugs. I didn't know adults could be so full of tears and hugs. My mother said, "And I no sooner come back and I see real honest *angels* in the sky! It's a sign! I know it is! Maybe we can be a real family now."

She said *family* like she meant it.

"Will you be taking our Bellflower away?" asked Great Aunt Twill, frightened. Her face looked like all the blood had suddenly drained out of it.

"You can't be thinking of taking Bellflower away from us!" cried Grams.

"To be truthful, Hollywood wasn't what I thought it would be," my mother said. "All those hoards and hoards of people, traffic and more traffic. Nobody cares if you live or don't in that place. I guess we'll be heading back to St. Paul."

"I've been thinking," said Skoot, who had been quiet until now. "Lake Clearbottom might could use a new beauty salon, Hollywood style."

"Say—Florence, honey," squealed Grams, excited, "Why don't you just settle right here in Lake Clearbottom and open you a beauty salon?"

"*Emporium*, you mean," said my mother. "A beauty emporium. I thought you'd never ask."

"And I'll design your emporium," said Tellride, casting her a long-lost cousin nod of encouragement.

"Would you like that, Bellflower?" my mother asked.

"Of *course* she'd like that!" shouted Great Aunt Twill grabbing me and hanging on to me for dear life. "She is loved here! Very much loved here! Isn't that true, Bellflower? Give us a hug!"

"Do I get my own room with a real bed?"

"Well, once I got established, I suppose I could even get you your own laptop like you've always wanted. Wireless. High speed. By the way, aren't you going to open the present I brought you?"

A large, heavy box sat on the floor by the Christmas tree. I tore open the wrapping and inside: the complete works of Charles Dickens.

Which goes to show that some stories do end up OK. People *do* find their authentic selves even if it was under their noses all along. And me, I can sure get used to waking up with no snow in my bed, and new books to read.

By the way, I gave my father's gold cross to my mother later that evening and she took one look at it and dissolved in a blanket of tears. She threw herself in Lady Mae's arms for comfort and they cried as though the accident had happened just two minutes ago.

I realized that's what people do when they lose someone they love. But we don't only lose people, we find people. When we *find* loved ones who have been lost, we hold on to them with all our might, and then we are happier than we ever thought we could be. And that's a fact.

Personal Private **KEEP OUT** this means YOU Journal

# Bellflower's Baked Ovaltine Strawberry Ice Cream Peanut Pie With Candy Canes Poking Out the Top

**For the crust:**
One ready-made graham cracker pie crust
1 Tablespoon Ovaltine powder
Sprinkle the crust with Ovaltine and bake 10 min.

**For the filling:**
½ gallon (or less) Strawberry Chunky ice cream
½ Cup Ovaltine powder
½ cup milk
1 Tablespoon butter or margarine
½ teaspoon Vanilla
1 Cup prepared whipping cream, like Cool Whip.
A handful of peanuts
4 or 5 miniature candy canes

Mix together the Ovaltine, milk butter and vanilla in a pan and heat, stirring, over the stove until it gets bubbly and melts. Scoop ice cream into the pie shell in a big happy mound. Pour the hot Ovaltine sauce over it. Sprinkle a few peanuts around on top. Put in freezer! When you're ready to serve, spread the whipping cream over it in heaps and then spread the rest of the peanuts on top. Poke the candy canes around.
Slice and serve. YUM!

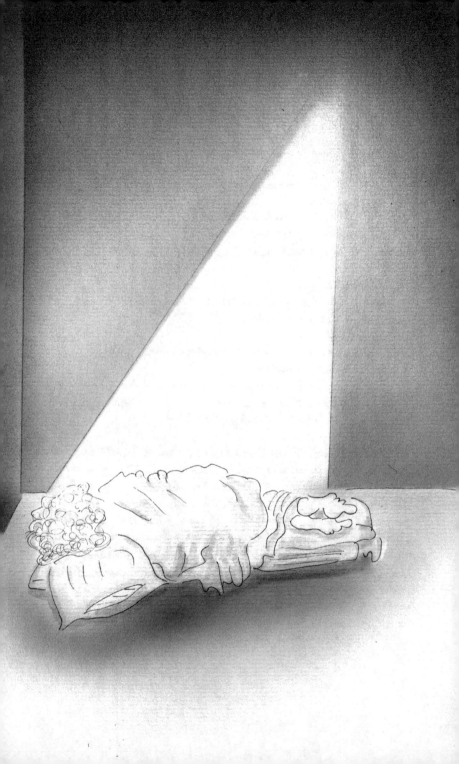

The End—probably.

Thought you'd like to see
more pages from my...

Personal Private **KEEP OUT** this means
*YOU* Journal

Hello
Person!

Me and scary tree.

YOU are a blessing!

Singing from my heart.

## Author and Illustrator
# MARIE CHAPIAN

Marie Chapian is one of the leading modern-day authorities on angels and supernatural phenomena. A Christian author of over 30 books and winner of the prestigious Gold Medallion award for her teen devotional, *Feeling Small, Walking Tall*, Marie has also written five children's books. Trained in Bible college and seminary, she also holds secular degrees in counseling, creative writing, and art. Marie is a Bible teacher and seminar speaker, and the experiences she writes about are based on actual experiences. You can find out more about Marie by visiting her Web site at www.mariechapian.com.

Other books by
# MARIE CHAPIAN
that *you* might like:

*Alula-Belle Blows Into Town*

*Alula-Belle Braves Ice Cream Beach*

## Books by MARIE CHAPIAN
that your parents might like:

*Angels In Our Lives*

*Telling Yourself the Truth*

*The Secret Place of Strength*

*Of Whom the World Was Not Worthy*

*Making His Heart Glad*

*God's Heart for You*

*The All-New Free To Be Thin*

*I Love You Like a Tomato*

*Mothers & Daughters*

Additional copies of this book and other
book titles from DESTINY IMAGE are
available at your local bookstore.

For a bookstore near you, call 1-800-722-6774.

Send a request for a catalog to:

**Destiny Image® Publishers, Inc.**
P.O. Box 310
Shippensburg, PA 17257-0310

*"Speaking to the Purposes of God for this
Generation and for the Generations to Come."*

**For a complete list of our titles,
visit us at www.destinyimage.com**